Only One Man Will Do

By
Fiona McGier

Eternal Press
A division of Damnation Books, LLC.
P.O. Box 3931
Santa Rosa, CA 95402-9998
www.eternalpress.biz

Only One Man Will Do
by Fiona McGier

Digital ISBN: 978-1-62929-081-2
Print ISBN: 978-1-62929-082-9

Cover art by: Amanda Kelsey
Edited by: Juanita Kees

Copyright 2013 Fiona McGier

Printed in the United States of America
Worldwide Electronic & Digital Rights
Worldwide English Language Print Rights

All rights reserved. No part of this book may be reproduced, scanned or distributed in any form, including digital and electronic or mechanical, including photocopying, recording, or by any information storage and retrieval system, without the prior written consent of the Publisher, except for brief quotes for use in reviews.

This book is a work of fiction. Characters, names, places and incidents either are the product of the author's imagination or are used fictitiously, and any resemblance to any actual persons, living or dead, events, or locales is entirely coincidental.

Praise for Fiona McGier's work:

"Ms. McGier's characters are realistically drawn, including a few secondary players who figure into the plot. Her location descriptions provide enough atmosphere without going overboard on details. The same can be noted about her sex scenes, which get the point across without being over explicit."
—Tim Smith, *Two Lips Reviews*

"Ms. McGier's book has a fast pace, believable characters and an interesting storyline. There are equal amounts of romance and suspense mixed in with frequent, spicy love scenes."
—Keitha Hart, *RT Book Reviews*

*To my readers,
who like reading about my alpha
heroines as much as I enjoy writing
them. Long-live beta heroes, especially
those who are alpha around the edges!*

Chapter One

"Damn that woman," Dmitri Illyanovich mumbled as he watched her get out of her SUV.

First came the high heels followed by the long length of shapely calves as she stretched her legs over the edge of the door. Her business-like skirt, normally conservatively knee-length, rode up to show her thighs clad in nylons, held up by... of all things, black garters. He shifted around in his seat, trying to stop his cock twitching like it had a mind of its own—as it did each time he caught a glimpse of her.

"This is business," he grumbled, reminding his errant body part to behave.

Dmitri had watched her for over a week to learn her movements. It took him a long time to find her, since all he had to go on from his cousin Ivan was that she was a biker queen, had bright red hair, huge tits and a nasty tendency to demand that things be done her way *or else*. He'd been in countless biker bars and bought beer for many unsavory characters. He'd even fought some of them when they made it clear how much they objected to a stranger with a Slavic accent asking questions about one of their own.

If he hadn't owed so much to his cousin Ivan for, among other things, helping him get into the United States, he might have given up. But Ivan wanted to give a wedding present to a good friend of his, and that gift involved first making sure that two drug dealers knew to stay away from the addiction-prone groom. The second part was ensuring that the biker queen, who had threatened to return someday to claim him for the night, knew that was something she should never attempt to do.

Finding and persuading the drug dealers was much easier. The groom, a famous action movie star, told him their names and even supplied their cell phone numbers. After that, it was only a matter of flying out to California and finding out where they lived. Once he did, he demonstrated graphically to each of them, how immensely painful it is for the human body when joints are forcibly dislodged. He'd watched as each of them deleted the name and phone number of the actor in question, and promised him they'd never contact him or any of his family ever again.

He'd driven each man in their own car, barely conscious and whimpering in pain, to the local hospital's emergency rooms and left them in the driveway. He assured them that after long enough in traction, they'd regain most of the feeling and use of the joints he'd stressed. That gave them plenty of time to think about how lucky they were his cousin hadn't asked him to kill them. He also told them that while he could find them again easily, there was no point in them going to the police to report him, because there was no record in this country of his existence. He'd be impossible to find, while they would be forcing him to have to find them again. And he would. That last part seemed to convince both of them he meant business.

But for the last part of the assignment, Dmitri had to use many of the skills he had picked up during the past twenty years to search for the elusive red-haired biker queen. Finally, he found someone who had ridden with her the night she tried to screw the actor his cousin wanted to protect. That biker was difficult to get information from, but Dmitri had learned a lot from Ivan, who had been in the KGB in its glory days. The man was a very reluctant informant, but talk he did, once Dmitri had made him understand that talking was preferable to enduring more torture.

The man had given Dmitri a name and the city she lived in…Alex Blackstone, Minneapolis, Minnesota. He said that was all he knew about her. It was enough for Dmitri to hack into the information systems that held phone numbers, addresses and vocations.

Armed with the appropriate data, he had driven to Minneapolis and located her, then began to track her movements to discover when he could be alone with her, to discuss how unwise it would be for her to ever try to force his cousin's friend to have sex with her.

The first few glimpses he got of her were enlightening. He had always had a weakness for redheads, and even though he wasn't sure if her hair color was natural or not, it suited her. She had the coloring for it, with pale skin covered with freckles. And with his cock insisting on becoming a rock each time he saw her, he asked himself why on earth the actor hadn't wanted to have sex with her. But that wasn't his concern. The actor was getting married and Ivan was giving him the gift of peace of mind, courtesy of his cousin.

Dmitri looked at his watch and sighed aloud. The woman had entered her office building and would go into her office to work while her secretary would head out to lunch. The time to act was now. He had already determined he wasn't going to dislocate any of the joints of her tantalizing body, but he still wasn't really sure how he was going to be able to influence her behavior. He had less than an hour to work with.

He opened the door of his car and got out.

Chapter Two

Alexandra Blackstone strode into her office purposefully. She sat down at her desk and pulled at some paperwork that needed to be reviewed. Once the file was in front of her, she opened it and began to read. Her inner observations reflected her opinion of the report.

They need a more forceful presence in the market...not sure we have the cajones to do it, but heard of our reputation. Hmm, wonder if they're worried because Daddy isn't in charge anymore? Yet another stupid man underestimating me because I've got a snatch?

She was already frowning in irritation when a noise from outside of her office made her look up.

Joyce was heading out to lunch as I walked in, so who's out there?

The door opened without anyone knocking and a mountain of a man walked through it without a word. Alexandra's eyes narrowed as she watched him move casually over to the chair on the opposite side of the desk and sat down with the supreme confidence of someone who knew he was expected.

"Who the fuck are you and what are you doing in my office?" She demanded.

The man studied her closely.

"Your voice is as low and sexy as I thought it would be, based on how you look." He made this observation casually, as if to himself.

Alexandra sat back and glared at him in silence to give herself time to think.

I don't feel threatened by him, but he's definitely a force to be reckoned with. He's not that tall, but he's built so wide it feels crowded in the office with just the two of us in it. I'll bet there's solid muscle under his clothes...

She frowned with irritation at her physical reaction as she studied the man who radiated alpha manhood at her while sitting still.

He's huge! I wonder what he's packing in those jeans. And

those shoulders look big enough to hold me down no matter how hard I fight...but why would I fight him when I already feel my juices beginning to leak out to soak my lacy black thong. He's waiting for me to make the next move.

"I repeat, who the fuck are you? I don't take any appointments at this time of day. I'm trying to catch up on paperwork. I don't have time to dick around with some asshole who pushes his way into my office. Should I call security and have you escorted out?"

His eyebrows rose and his lips turned up slightly. "You could try. That would give me a reason to come around to your side of the desk."

The curve of his lips suggested he found the idea appealing. His eyes grew darker, hinting he wanted her to give him a reason to get out of his chair. She tried not to draw attention as she squirmed in her chair.

Shit! He's got sexy dimples when he smiles. His dark brown eyes are so piercing I feel like he's stripped me in his mind and he's got me bent over the desk already! He must be putting out some powerful pheromones to get me so hot so quickly. Either that or it's been way too long since I got laid...

He cleared his throat to get her attention.

"We need to talk, Alexandra Blackstone. I have a message for you."

She leaned forward and rested her arms on the desk, tapping steepled forefingers against each other—a habit she'd learned from her dad to show this man he had her full attention.

"What is that message?"

"You need to stay away from Raul Roderick. You're not to contact him or any of his family, nor are you to attempt to collect on a threat you made to him that you would find him someday and make him...*ahem*...make him have sex with you."

Alexandra leaned back and laughed.

"I think you have me confused with someone else. I don't know what you're talking about."

He leaned forward and Alexandra felt the air being pushed toward her, like his tiniest movements were affecting her surroundings.

Shit! He's radiating heat like a volcano! I'm sweating...but so's he. The closer he gets, the more I smell aroused-man-hormones, so he's not immune. Hmm, maybe that can be useful.

"Oh, I think you do. You are Alexandra Blackstone, daughter of Thomas Blackstone who founded this marketing company. He had two daughters, no son. You are the elder so you are the one he groomed to take over his business when he retired, which he did last year. He still sits on the board when he's not tanning in Florida."

She found it difficult to concentrate on his words when even his voice was affecting her, making her nipples pucker while a tingle began to run through her body, creating heat in her abdomen. She clamped her upper thighs together and frowned.

"All of which is public record. None of which suggests I know what the hell you're talking about."

He leaned back with a smile and crossed his legs, his right ankle resting on his left thigh, giving her a good view of the large bulge in his crotch area. She tried to ignore her body's reaction as her inner muscles tensed in anticipation. Her nipples beaded against the lacy bra, the moisture between her thighs seeped onto her thong and her breathing sped up as she imagined what was stretching the fabric. She looked up to focus on something…anything else, and found herself staring at wide fingers resting on the arms of the chair. She blinked in surprise.

Jesus, his cock must be wider than my wrist! He looks like he knows what I'm thinking. He's toying with me, damn him. And he's enjoying it.

"You are also Alex, the red-headed biker queen of a group of Harley riders based out of the Mille Lacs area. You spend your weekends up there during riding weather, staying at a farmhouse owned by your family, surrounded by the gang you recruited personally. You fuck all the men and keep everyone in line by the sheer force of your personality."

He studied her intently making her feel naked under his gaze. She squirmed again as the wetness grew. *Damn! I'll have to get my suit dry-cleaned after this!*

She attempted to bluff. "I don't know what you're talking about. Since I have work to do, I suggest you leave now, mister…what was your name?"

"There's no need for lying between us, Alexandra." Her name rolled off his tongue to caress her in places she tried to ignore. "We are two of a kind. Like you, I wear many faces, many names. I don't have a public identity for you to search out. I make no judgments. I'm speaking to you plainly because I won't insult your intelligence by lying. I've been sent by my cousin to do a favor for the actor I mentioned. He's getting married and has given up his drug-fueled lifestyle. He's making a clean break with his past in order to build a future with his bride. I promised my cousin I'd make sure the drug dealers who used to supply him knew to stay away from him. I used…shall we say…some carefully applied persuasion. Once they get out of the hospital I don't think they'll try to contact him again. You are the last name on my list. Once I've convinced you to drop any claim you might feel you had on him, I can tell my cousin I'm done."

He's not here trying to seduce me? He's only here to give me an ultimatum? What balls! Maybe he thinks because he's so alpha I'll agree to anything? Who the fuck does he think he is?

She felt her anger rising, the familiar redness rising in her face, her skin heating up as she realized this man thought *he* could order *her* around.

"What? Did *he* send you after me? Is that big movie star too much of a pussy to take care of business himself?"

He shook his head. "No, but as I told you, my cousin is giving him *peace of mind* as a wedding gift. Once you agree not to cause him any further trouble, our business is done and I will leave."

Alexandra took a few deep breaths to force her anger and her raging hormones under her control.

I've done this before. Negotiating a win-win situation is one of my specialties.

She studied him carefully, making sure he noticed her staring at the bulge in his pants she swore twitched under her gaze. Her eyes rose up his torso as she imagined the muscular barrel-shaped chest under his shirt, and the wide shoulders that looked like he'd have no trouble holding her down. She looked up and into his eyes and was gratified and excited by the naked lust on his face.

"Okay, Russian…you *are* Russian aren't you? Your Slavic accent seems to get more pronounced when you're…excited…" She nodded towards his erection, licked her lips and smiled.

He nodded as his nostrils flared and his eyes narrowed.

He knows we're in negotiations. Her nerves thrummed with anticipation.

He cleared his throat. "My name is Dmitri."

"Okay, Dmitri. You're right. I *am* the woman you're looking for. And you're also right about us being two of a kind. You'll have to forgive me for trying to play games with you, but I'm wearing a suit and sitting in my office. I have to pretend to be all kinds of things to win the endless power plays involved with being a woman running a man's business."

He nodded again, his gaze so heated she felt about to burst into flames.

"So...if I agree to your terms...and I'm not saying I will... but if I agree, what do I get in return? I presume you aren't going to put me in hospital if I don't."

"Why not?"

She shook her head, "Because I don't get the vibe off of you that you would hurt a woman."

"I have. I might again. But continue."

She tried not to show how his words sent a tremor of excitement that made her already primed body want to explode.

"I ask again...what do I get if I agree?"

His nostrils flared again as he inhaled deeply.

"What do you want?"

You bastard! You can smell how excited I am, can't you?

"I wanted bragging rights for having fucked the famous Raul Roderick. But I'm willing to forget the whole celebrity-whore thing for a good hard dicking from a big, powerful Russian man."

A slow smile spread across his face. Combined with the lust already there, it made him look like a predator about to take down his prey. She tensed her body in anticipation.

He pushed himself up and moved around the desk as she watched him. He strolled casually around the far edge, staring into her eyes as he rounded the first corner. His eyes traveled down her face to her neck before dropping lower. As he rounded the nearer corner, he studied the swell of each breast as if he could burn off the clothing that kept them covered. He licked his lips in anticipation.

Breathe, Alex, breathe! My heart's racing so fast I'll pass out without oxygen. He moves just like a panther stalking and I'm the prey!

He stood next to her chair and reached out to push on the

backrest to bring her face to face with him. He stared into her eyes as she tried not to pant. A vein throbbed on the side of his neck,

Good, his heart's racing too.

After a long moment, he inclined his head toward the desk, still holding her gaze.

"Nice desk. Looks pretty sturdy."

"It was my father's desk."

"And now it's yours. Sit on the edge of the desk, Alexandra, so I can sit on the chair."

"Now you think you can order me around?"

His lips twitched.

"*Please* seat yourself on the edge of the desk, so I can sit on the chair."

She rose slowly, still staring into his eyes to show she was only obeying because she wanted to see what he would do next, not because she had to. She turned to slide her butt across the cool surface, pushing aside the forgotten papers. Her skirt rode up as she slid back, thighs parted as an invitation.

He sat down on the chair and moved closer. His hands stroked her knees for a moment, trailed slowly up her thighs and began to caress the bare skin above the garters. His fingers stroked the tender skin gently, moving upwards to the crease at the top of her thighs. Both thumbs pushed against her labia as he pressed them together to allow him to feel how hard her clit had become.

A small sound escaped her involuntarily and he looked up to see her watching him and growled. With a quick flick of his wrists, he ripped through both sides of the thong at once. She heard the elastic snap, felt the momentary pain as the thong bit into the skin of her hips before it was ripped from her body and thrown to the floor.

Dmitri leaned closer and inhaled slowly. "Ah, that's better. Now you are all I can smell."

He pushed her skirt further up, baring her legs and her pussy. His thumbs rubbed the sensitive skin at the crease of her thighs while his fingers moved the skirt out of his way. There was a low murmur of approval.

"And you *are* a natural redhead. This just gets better and better..."

Alexandra leaned back on her desk, her hands near her hips, her shoulders beginning to ache from the strain of holding herself in place so tightly.

"When is it going to get better for me?" She tried not to sound as eager as she felt, but damn it, this man had her so hot she was ready to scream!

She thought she heard a low chuckle but then he leaned forward and the tip of his tongue flicked across her clit. Thinking became impossible. She moaned. His tongue began to explore, the tip dipping into her slit, spreading her juices. He leaned closer and pressed his mouth against her mound, humming while his teeth grazed her throbbing clit.

Alexandra screamed as she came, shaking and quivering with the sudden relaxation of the tight hold she'd had on her muscles. She squeezed her eyes shut and watched the starbursts on her eyelids.

She felt herself pulled closer to the edge of the desk and his thick, wide cock spread pre-come on her briefly. He pushed into her and she screamed again as he filled her, her muscles clamping down, her clit rubbed by the length as he buried himself to the hilt. She came again, the stars exploding on her field of vision.

Dmitri grunted when he was completely inside of her, pulled back then surged forward with another grunt. He continued this rhythm, his wideness stretching her to the point of pain, before he pulled out and entered her again.

Alexandra's arms began to shake with the strain of holding herself up, but she was unable to move any part of herself other than the muscles that clamped down on his wide cock each time it filled her until his balls slapped against her. Dmitri reached up to place one hand on each side of her blouse and he pulled. Buttons flew off as he tore the front open, then pinched her nipples through her black lacy bra.

"*Yes.*" Alexandra moaned as his fondling of her nipples provided one last ingredient for multiple-orgasmic bliss. He pulled the fronts of the bra down and her breasts spilled over the top. His large hands palmed and squeezed the sensitive skin as he continued to twist the large nipples between his thumbs and forefingers. She pushed against him harder and faster, feeling him speeding up, the only sound in the office the brutal slapping of skin against skin as they both sought the same goal.

She knew it was close…she could feel the blood beginning to pound in her ears. He moved to one side and drove her over the edge. She let out a long, loud wail as her world exploded in fireworks, shattering her consciousness into a million pieces as she rode his cock to one earth-shaking orgasm after another.

"Aargh!" He howled as he pulled her tightly against him to hold her with hands of steel. His fingers dug into her hips making bruises that would surely leave their marks for weeks.

He continued to pulse forcefully into her, each blast of hot come making her spiral into another orgasm. She felt him twitch inside of her and squeezed tighter to keep him coming until, after a few long moments, he fell backwards onto the chair, still holding her tightly on his hips. As he hit the seat, she felt gravity push her down onto him, his still-throbbing cock slamming into her even deeper than before. She squeaked out another small orgasm, quivered then collapsed onto his chest. She wrapped her arms around his shoulders and sighed.

His barrel chest and wide shoulders meant she felt tiny nestled on his chest. Alexandra was a tall woman, and usually men had to be well over six feet for her to feel small. Dmitri wasn't much taller than her but he was sturdy and wide.

Every part of him is wide! I have a new favorite dick! She smiled.

When they could both breathe again, Alexandra licked along his neck, watching the vein beginning to throb on the side again. She trailed the tip of her tongue up along his jaw, then stopped to look into his eyes, her face right in front of his.

"Not bad for a first installment," she said with a grin. "What do you do for an encore?"

His cock twitched inside of her as he pushed forward and drew back a few times. She moaned as she crashed into some after-shocks. When she could think again she spoke.

"I think we should go to my condo. I want to see what you can do when we are both naked. And I want more space to move around in. I wonder how many times you can come in one night."

He chuckled. "More than most men, but not more than you, sexy lady. I love a woman who is so responsive she can come repeatedly and quickly. Taking my time with you is going to be a pleasure."

Her face and tone became serious. "Just so's you know, I had my yearly checkup this week. I'm disease-free and I have an IUD, so I won't get pregnant."

He nodded, "So that's what I'm feeling." He moved again and she squeezed him tightly with muscles honed by years of kegel exercises.

"I got a medical check when I got to America and I don't remember the last time I rode bareback."

Her lips curled in amusement. "I'm surprised you can find condoms to fit around yourself. You're not the biggest cock I've ever ridden, but you sure are the widest. I think I have a new favorite."

He nodded. "Good. Me too. It's not often I find a woman who can come quickly, yet keep going for as long as I can hold on. I'm looking forward to finding out what we're capable of doing together with more time."

"So let's get going right now," she pulled herself up and off of his lap.

He watched her move around the desk, to peer into the mirror on the back of the door.

"I think we'd better leave through the back door. Joyce is a good secretary, but I've known her since I was a little girl. She doesn't need to see me looking like this."

She felt him moving behind her. She was going to turn but he pushed her over so she was bent over the back of the leather couch. He pushed himself into her again as she groaned.

He spoke into her ear, his hot breath blowing on the tiny hairs on her neck, making her quiver as he filled her again. He reached one arm around her and fingered her clit.

"You mean looking like you just got a good fucking? And like you are going to get some more?"

"Yes!" Her teeth gnashed as she came again.

He chuckled against her neck and ear.

"Come, my lady Alexandra. We have hours to go before we sleep."

He pulled back from her and she turned, grinning. She pulled her skirt back down, and pushed her breasts back into their holders. Turning to the mirror she buttoned the few buttons left on her blouse, and pushed the tendrils of hair that had come out of her up-do back behind her ears.

Behind her, she watched in the mirror as Dmitri gingerly closed his zipper over what was still a massive erection.

"I wonder…will that ever go down completely?" She asked with a smile.

"Probably not while you're around. But maybe. We'll see."

She walked past him to push on the intercom button, "Joyce?"

"Yes, Ms. Blackstone?"

"I'm going to call it a day. Please reschedule my late afternoon appointment."

"Yes, Ms. Blackstone. And if your father calls?"

"Um, tell him something important...uh...came up." She smiled as Dmitri made stroking motions in front of his groin.

"And I'll see you Monday morning. Have a good weekend."

"Thank-you, Ms. Blackstone. And you also."

Alexandra turned to the man who had insinuated himself into her life so abruptly and smiled. He held out a hand and took hers, then kissed the back of her fingers.

"Ready?" He asked her.

"Am I ever!" She said breathily. At his questioning look, she grinned. "That means yes."

She led the way to the back entrance to her office and down the stairs. When they got to her car, she turned to him. "Where's your car?"

He smiled. "It's a rental. I travel light. I'll deal with getting it back to them once we're done."

"Do you mean on Monday, after breakfast, when you ride back here with me?"

He nodded. "*Da.*"

Chapter Three

Alexandra groaned when her cell phone rang. She was held firmly in place next to a mountain of a man, and the sound didn't seem to be bothering him at all. Certainly he didn't relax his hold on her. She squirmed, trying to wake him enough to get him to let her move.

"Hey, big guy! That ring-tone means it's my dad calling. Let me up so I can see what he wants."

She pushed at his arm until she'd made herself enough of an opening for her to slide down underneath it, then stumbled out of bed to locate the purse she'd flung onto the dresser on their way into the bedroom.

After the sixth ring the phone will go to voicemail. Dad will be majorly pissed if I don't pick up his call, especially at this time of the morning!

"I wonder what the fuck time it is, anyway," she mumbled as she dug her phone out and touched it to answer it as it began the sixth ring.

Dmitri rolled over to watch her as she stood talking on the phone.

She's magnificent! Miles of milky white skin, covered with freckles. Red curls covering her mound, nicely trimmed, but still there. She's not one of those modern women who think a hairless little-girl's pussy is attractive. Though for her I'd make an exception.

As if she felt him ogling her, she turned to wink at him as she listened. He stared at the large, reddish nipples atop her mountainous breasts.

And they're real. No implants for this woman...she doesn't need them. Those silver-dollar nipples almost fill my mouth. And responsive? God, what a woman!

He looked up and with a start, realized that even though she was still talking to her father, she was staring at the cock that was already hard and dripping again, as if it hadn't come repeatedly all night long. They had passed out from exhaustion after hours of fucking in every possible position either of them could think of, as well as a few they thought up together.

"Okay, Dad. I got it. I'll see you at the Club at four. I know you want me to meet the father of the man who's running the business. I still think it's weird you think the old man will be more impressed by my abilities than the younger one, but if you say so..." She nodded and said, "See you at four." Then she flung the phone onto the dresser and nodded at Dmitri.

"I'm going to make a quick visit to the bathroom. You can use the one down the hall to your right. Then I'll see what I can do about that enormous hard-on of yours." She licked her lips and smiled, went through and closed the door behind her.

He smiled and got up to make his way down the hall to find the bathroom. When he got out he listened for a moment, then headed in the direction the noises were coming from. Alexandra was putting cream cheeses on the small kitchen table, next to the bag of bagels. The sounds were coming from the coffee pot. Dmitri's stomach growled to remind him that it had been many hours since they'd split the pizza she'd ordered when they were resting up in-between bouts of acrobatic sex. They had soaked in the Jacuzzi while the food digested, then moved back onto the bed for more wild fucking.

"What time is it, anyway?" Dmitri asked as he approached her, grabbing her hips and rubbing himself in the cleft between her ass cheeks as she reached in the fridge for the milk.

She obligingly wiggled her ass, making his cock twitch, then turned and with the milk in one hand, she pulled at the back of his neck with the other, to get him to kiss her. They were almost the same height, barefoot, so it was easy to lean forward and cover her lips with his. He poked her lips with his tongue and she opened her mouth to let him taste the toothpaste she'd brushed with in the bathroom.

"You cheated," he said, aggrieved. "I only got to rinse my mouth with water."

"Maybe you should leave a toothbrush here," she said lightly as she turned to put the milk on the counter. She poured coffee into two cups and turned again to put them both onto the table. She gestured at the chair on the side further away from the fridge.

"Sit. Have some coffee and bagels. I presume you heard my conversation with my dad?"

He took a small sip of the coffee and finding it too hot, poured some milk into it, and took another sip. He waited until she was done slicing open a bagel before taking the knife and picking a poppy-seed one for himself.

"I was too busy staring at your tits," he said with a grin. "Though I did hear something about you going to meet him at four?"

She chewed slowly. "Yeah. The paperwork on my desk that we fucked on was from some prospective new client who's not sure I have the balls to do the kind of work he wants done. My dad never got that kind of shit from anyone. He built his company on the reputation of being able to play on the big dogs' playground and win."

Dmitri shrugged as he took a big bite, then spoke around it.

"Some men don't think women are able to be as tough as they think *they* are," he observed. "I, on the other hand, learned from an early age that some women have twice the balls of the men around them, and they can use that to their advantage. The men who underestimate them never see it coming." He grinned.

Alexandra nodded, "Exactly my point. You're right...we really are two of a kind, honey."

He shook his head as he swallowed, "We have a few differences I noticed last night. *Viva la difference!*"

Her lips curled upwards.

"So the upshot is after we eat, and have some more hot, monkey sex, I have to get into my business clothes again and go make nice with my dad, and the guy he's making his new golfing buddy, today at the indoor range. That way when I meet with the son on Monday, he'll have already been chewed a new asshole by *his* dad, and I'll get the job whether he thinks I can do it or not."

Dmitri took a big swallow of his coffee before he spoke.

"Does this mean you're throwing me out after breakfast and..." his dark eyes glittered like coals, "...more world-class fucking?"

Alexandra leaned back in her chair and sipped her coffee slowly. "Depends. The only plan I have is to meet Dad. I'll only be there for a couple of hours. After that I'd like to grab some dinner, then go hit some biker bars. I get antsy this time of year, when I can't just hop on my bike and ride. I hate having to ride on four wheels to go party, but it's impossible to stay on the road on a Harley with this much snow and ice. I hate March! I'm tired of cold and snow!"

"Are you inviting me to tag along?"

Her hazel eyes sparkled with amusement, "Do you think you're up for it? I'm well-known in the places I hang out in. The guys will want to test you, to be sure you're good enough for me. You might end up in a few fights before the night is over."

He poured himself more coffee and after stirring milk into it, looked deeply into her eyes.

"Will the night be over after the bars? Or am I invited to once again share your bed? Or is that what you expect I'll be fighting for, when the other bikers are *testing* me?"

Alexandra laughed. "You're really something, you know that? No, the night won't be over after the bars. And yes, you'll be tested by other men I've fucked to be sure they think you're good enough to deserve me. You can pretty much assume I've had most of the men in the bars. I've been riding with my gang for a long time. I handpick who's allowed to ride with me."

He nodded. "The women too?"

Her eyes narrowed. "Are you asking me if I swing both ways?"

"I might be," he said casually.

"Why? You wanna watch?"

"Watching someone else make you come is not my idea of a good time," he growled as he got up. He moved quickly to stand in front of her and pulled her hands to get her to stand up. One hand quickly moved behind her to cup her butt cheek, pressing her into his cock. His other hand tweaked her nipple then trailed up her neck to rest under her chin, forcing her to look into his eyes.

"Don't you like to share?" She felt like she was poking at a dangerous animal when he growled again, shaking his head slowly.

"No!"

His hand moved back into her hair to pull her head forward as he crushed her lips with his. She whimpered as he moved his hips back to allow him to force his cock between her legs. She squeezed her upper thighs together, feeling him harden even more.

"Bedroom?" Her voice was a hoarse croak, her throat raspy from panting.

They only made it as far as the living room before he bent her over the back of the couch and eased himself into her again. She felt him stretching her, inch by incredible inch, while she wriggled her ass, enjoying feeling all of her inner muscles being stroked by his girth.

Once he was firmly planted in her, he leaned forward over her back and reached around to fondle her breasts, rolling her nipples between his thumbs and forefinger, pulling them down with each hard thrust of his hips.

Alexandra shrieked as she came, feeling herself clamp down on him, squeezing him so tightly she could feel the veins pulsating in his cock. She felt bereft as he pulled himself all of the way out of her before nudging her backwards onto the couch, one of her legs still draped over the back of it. He moved quickly to stand in front of her, pulling her other leg around his hips as he teased her with the pre-cum leaking out of him before pushing himself into her again. The angle was different, allowing for him to fill her more completely. She looked up at his face set in a grimace as he increased the speed of his thrusts, slamming himself into her then pulling out and pushing back in again before she could catch her breath.

She felt it building quickly, her moans getting closer together as she neared the point of no return. Suddenly she froze. One more thrust, once more again, and she shattered into a million pieces as she came.

"Aah!"

Dmitri grunted once more then held her against him and filled her with his hot cum, the spurting so forceful she could almost taste it. With a final groan he collapsed forward onto her.

They lay still, their bodies relearning how to breathe normally as their heartbeats slowed gradually. Alexandra felt her body twitch as she rode the aftershocks of pleasure.

When she could speak again, she asked, "Are you ever going to get tired?"

She felt his chest rumble as he chuckled from deep in his throat.

"Of you? Never!"

"I feel all sticky. We should get up and shower," she observed.

He pushed himself up to hold onto the back of the couch with one hand as he slowly eased his hips away from her, his cock still partly erect as it slid out of her with a *pop*. He moved further up and grasped her hands to pull her up and off of the couch, before he enfolded her in his arms for a long moment of a bear hug.

She turned her head up questioningly and looked into his face.

Oh, my God! Why's he looking at me like that? What the fuck?

"Dude," she began with a warning tone in her voice. The fleeting look she had seen disappeared so quickly she wondered if she had imagined it.

"I need a shower and to get dressed before I run some Saturday errands."

He nodded, "I'm going to get some food for tomorrow morning's breakfast."

Her eyes widened. "You are? Why?"

"Because bagels and fruit might be enough for a woman, but I need a more substantial breakfast to keep my strength up. I especially need a massive dose of protein, after all of the bodily fluids I've been producing for you."

She grinned. "Well that's fine...as long as you don't expect me to cook it for you. Boiling water for tea or making coffee is about all I'm good for in the kitchen. I grew up in a house with a maid and a cook."

He nodded. "That explains the lack of anything edible in your fridge."

At her surprised look he explained, "When you opened it to put the milk and cream cheese away, I glanced into it and wondered what you do for food."

She sniffed. "That's what phones and delivery are for. Or I go out to eat."

"I think I'll get some steaks for dinner also. Do I need to pick up the wine too?"

She shook her head. "Ah...no. I might not have any food ingredients around, but I know a lot about wine. It's one of the things my dad taught me so I could impress clients with my *savoir faire* about *vino*."

They walked down the hall to the huge master bathroom with the shower built for multiple occupants.

"Remember I told you I want to grab something quick on

our way to the biker bars tonight," she began as she turned on the water to heat it up for their shower.

"Fine. I'll take care of tomorrow's meals. Breakfast and dinner."

"No lunch?"

She was stepping under the water when he pressed himself against her backside, his hands reaching forward to fondle her breasts as he growled at her.

"I don't intend to let you out of bed for breakfast until long after the sun comes up. There won't be time for lunch. And after we work that food off, you'll be ready to eat a steak dinner prepared Russian-style."

She sighed as his fingers stroked her insistently until with a surprised squeak, she came again.

"If you don't stop doing that, we'll never get out of here," she chided him.

A slow smile spread across his face.

"I'm just making sure you'll be anxious to get back here later tonight."

Her eyebrows rose. "And what if I find a better man in the bar?"

He shook his head. "There's no better man for you."

With that he began to rub her scalp, letting the water soak her head, then applying shampoo and working it into a lather. As she felt her skin relax under his fingers, she sighed.

"You may be right."

Unseen by her, he smiled.

Chapter Four

They had arranged for him to be back at her building's parking lot by 5:30 p.m. When she pulled into her spot, she looked around for him but didn't see his rental car.

He's late. Whatever. I've got to get out of these clothes. It's a Saturday night, for Christ's sake! My skin needs to breathe.

As she approached the door of her condo she dug her key out of her purse. She put it into the lock and let herself in. She turned to lock the door again and realized someone was in the room with her. She whirled around to see Dmitri standing in the doorway leading to her kitchen.

"How the hell did you get in here?" She tried to keep her voice from shaking, though she wasn't sure if it was with fear or anger...or both.

He shrugged. "I learned a lot of things from my cousin, but getting through locked doors wasn't one of them. That I learned myself, when I was just a kid."

"This place is a high security building. I pay a lot for that service."

He smirked. "So? Very few can let themselves in, as I did. It's worth the money to keep out most people. I'm not *most people*."

Irritated, she snapped, "Fine. Note to self: new man can break into any high security establishment. Could be useful."

He watched her closely as she tossed her coat onto the couch.

"I've got to get into some weekend clothes."

"Is that why you told me to wear jeans?"

She nodded, eyeing the black leather bomber jacket on the dining room table.

"Yeah. Good choice with the jacket. And the boots. We're going to be in some rough places. You're going to be tested just because you're with me. You don't want them to think you're a pussy."

He barked out a laugh.

"I can't think of the last man who called me that…not one who is still alive, at any rate."

She glanced back at him over her shoulder as she headed into her bedroom to change.

"I don't know whether I should believe you or not."

His lips twitched. "Your choice."

Almost two hours later, Alexandra pulled into a spot that looked too small for her SUV, and parked partially on a snow bank. Light and noise streamed out of the door of the bar each time someone went in or out. They had stopped for a quick burger and fries at a small local diner along the way. Dmitri studied how she was changing before his eyes, becoming less the polished businesswoman and more the edgy biker queen Ivan had sent him to deal with.

This is going to be a rough ride. At some point I'm going to have to decide if this wildcat's worth the trouble. For now, I'm leaning towards yes.

With that he followed her up to the entrance, past the few bikes tricked out to deal with the incessant snow and ice of Minnesota winters. She pushed open the door to show him her other self.

She was recognized at once. There were calls to her from many of the people in the place. She pulled Dmitri by the hand as she smoothly made her way over to the bar, smiling and nodding at those who called her name as she passed.

Once at the bar she grabbed the beer the bartender had already poured for her and downed half of it in one long gulp. She turned and acknowledged the cheers with a loud belch before she delicately licked the foam off her upper lip.

"Hey guys! It's been too long, right? I want you all to meet the owner of my new favorite cock. His name is Dmitri and he's Russian. And man, does he know about keeping this woman happy!"

She made a big show out of adjusting her skin-tight jeans.

"It's hard to keep my clothes on when he's around. But since this here is a family place," she laughed along with the loud yelling and catcalls that greeted those words, "I'll try to keep my pants on…for now."

She waved her hand at the people who were sitting close to or at the bar. "These here are my people, Dmitri. I've hand-picked who rides with me," she winked at her riders then leered at them, "And it wasn't just my hand I used to pick the best ones!"

More loud laughter. Alexandra turned to Dmitri, "So what are you drinking?"

The bartender was already pushing another beer towards her almost empty glass.

"Wodka," he said in a loud, gruff voice.

Some of the men's eyebrows rose and one of the women yelled out, "Better be careful with that stuff! With you drinking the hard stuff and her drinking beer, you try matching her drink-for-drink and she'll have to drag you home behind her bike...after you fall off!"

Dmitri smiled at her, making a big show out of admiring her tight jeans and halter top that exposed more than it covered.

"Didn't you hear? I'm Russian. We start out drinking wodka in our baby bottles. Besides," he inclined his head towards Alexandra who was already drinking her second beer. "American beer is piss. No flavor and no kick. I'll stick with my national drink."

There was some laughter and some jeers after his words. One of the men strode over to stand right in front of Dmitri, so close to him that the others grabbed their drinks off the table in case someone was going to be punched and fall over in their direction.

"So, the Ruski don't like American beer? Maybe I don't like Ruskis," the man growled at Dmitri, arms at his side, his hands curling into fists.

Alexandra watched them silently, still sipping her beer.

Dmitri breathed deeply which seemed to make every cell in his body expand. He looked like he was growing in size, until the other man took an inadvertent step back.

"That's okay, dude. I don't like hot dogs or apple pie much either. Don't mean I don't like being in America. Your Mama just dropped you here. I chose to come here. It's a big country. There's plenty of room for all of us."

He turned to nod at Alexandra, "And you have some of the best-looking women in the world."

The man growled as he moved forward with his right fist pulled back, and two things happened simultaneously.

Alexandra said in a loud voice, "Stand down, Jim! He's under my protect—"

Before she finished the word, Dmitri's arm flashed forward so quickly it was a blur. No one actually saw what part of him connected with the other man, or where, but Jim staggered backwards. Two men standing behind him grabbed him to hold him upright as he turned dark red, choking in a breath.

Dmitri turned back to the bartender and pointed at his shot glass. As more vodka was poured into his glass, Alexandra spoke sharply.

"What did you do? Why can't he breathe?"

"His diaphragm will spasm for a while. Eventually he'll be able to breathe again. It will be quicker if he passes out. But he'll be fine."

The men holding him up eased Jim over to a nearby empty chair and pushed him over into it. His head lolled back as his eyes shut. Suddenly his chest expanded quickly and he let out the air with a whooshing sound, and normal breathing resumed. He opened his eyes to stare around him, as if he had just woken up.

Alexandra punched Dmitri in the upper arm.

"That's not fair! He was just testing you! You could've just hit him, or punched him. The guys like to fight. They spar with each other all the time. You didn't have to really hurt anyone."

Dmitri shrugged and pointed at the rapidly recovering offender who was reaching his hand out to grab the beer he was being offered.

"I don't like to spar. I don't like to fight. When I get pushed hard enough, I will. But I don't hold back." He looked away from her to glance around at the bikers she rode with and spoke slightly louder, "So if you don't want to get hurt, don't mess with me. Let me drink in peace and quiet."

He got up from the bar stool and walked over to the table where Jim was just putting his beer back down. He offered his right hand.

"No harm, no foul. Right?"

Jim seemed to consider that before he held out his right hand, saying in a harsh, raspy tone, "Sure. No hard feelings. Welcome to the gang, Dmitri."

"Yeah, it'll be good to know we have you on our side the next time we really do get into it with some other gang. I'm Rich."

One of the men who had caught the errant Jim, moved over to shake Dmitri's hand also. "I'm Bob. Pleased to meetcha."

They all gave their names as they shook with him, and Alexandra watched closely as the females moved over to kiss him, each one rubbing herself on his chest, each one insinuating how much she'd enjoy getting to know him better.

"That's enough," she said sharply as a diminutive blonde reached her hands around the back of him to grab his ass while rubbing her nipples on his chest.

"Didn't you hear me, Katie? He's my new favorite. You know the rules. Hands off until I'm done keeping him to myself. If he lasts," she turned and leered at Dmitri, "you can get in line for what's left when I'm ready to share."

She looked up and around at the rest of the patrons in the bar, many of whom had stopped talking to watch.

"Show's over! Mind your own fucking business or I'll sic him on you, too!"

The noise level resumed as the other drinkers turned their backs or resumed their darts and pool games. Now that there wasn't any imminent danger of large, flying male bodies knocking over glasses anymore, the partying went back to normal.

Alexandra took another long drink from her beer. One of the men yelled over from the newly vacant table and asked Dmitri if he wanted to shoot pool. He looked over at her and their eyes met.

"Go ahead," she said.

"I wasn't asking your permission," he growled.

Her eyebrows rose as she raked him with her eyes.

"No, I guess you wouldn't."

He got up and walked over to the pool table to examine the cues, and find the least warped one possible.

The short blonde sat on the barstool next to Alexandra and smiled at her.

"Is he as good as that bulge in his pants promises?"

Alexandra nodded without smiling. "Uh-huh."

"You think you're gonna be ready to share soon?"

She continued to stare at Dmitri, watching him closely as he bent over to make a shot. There was a noisy intake of breath from the blonde as his jeans appeared molded to his ass, now on display for both of them.

"Uh-uh," she said. "That ass is mine until I'm tired of it."

The blonde shrugged, "Okay, fine. You never stay interested in any of them for long. I can wait. It'll build my anticipation, ya know?" She licked her lips. "And I'll really enjoy it when I get to see him in action when we start staying at your place again." She sighed. "I really miss your playroom in the barn. Good hard fucking is fine, but there's nothing like being able to prolong it with handcuffs and toys."

Alexandra regarded Dmitri thoughtfully. "Somehow I doubt he's going to want to be a part of that." She turned to look at the other woman whose eyes had widened in surprise. "He doesn't do sharing. We'll have to see what I can talk him into when the weather gets nicer."

"Hey Katie, bring us another pitcher, will ya?" One of the guys playing darts waved to indicate their empty glasses. "We're parched over here!"

The blonde smiled and nodded at him, grabbing the pitcher the bartender slid towards her. She swung her hips as she sashayed over to them, and grabbed the butt of the guy who had yelled at her.

"Here's your beer, Chuck. And remember, I get to fuck the winner."

"What if there's a tie?"

She wriggled in anticipation, "Then I'll fuck both of ya."

Loud male laughter greeted that and the darts game continued with renewed vigor.

Many hours later Dmitri tongue-kissed Alexandra while the lights were flashing. The bartender loudly announced he was really serious this time. "Closing time is 3:00 a.m. folks. I'm not risking another ticket for being open too long."

Alexandra leaned into the kiss, enjoying the feel of Dmitri's hands on her, promising so much more once they were back in her condo. When he drew back he dangled her keys in front of her.

"I'm driving," he announced.

She shook her head. "You prick! That's why you were grabbing my ass? To steal my keys? No one drives my SUV."

"Then I won't be going home with you, because you're too sloppy drunk to drive." He shook his head. "That's what cheap beer does to you."

She glared at him through glassy eyes, before finally nodding her head.

"If I let you drive, do you promise to fuck me silly once we get back?"

His eyebrows rose, while his lips twitched in amusement.

"I mean, when I'm this drunk I like it good and hard. Fuck me with that big hard cock of yours until I pass out from pleasure, okay? You promise me that and you can drive."

"I don't usually take advantage of women who've had too much to drink. But in your case, since you're begging me so nicely, I'll make an exception."

She grabbed at his crotch and rubbed his cock, smiling as it hardened in her hand. "Drive fast."

And he did.

It wasn't too much longer after they had gotten back to her condo that she passed out. They had stripped on the way down the hall, and torn at each other like wild animals once they got to the bedroom. Dmitri made sure Alexandra was wailing out multiple orgasms before he finally let himself go.

Soon after that, he lay on his back catching his breath, holding her in his arms while she was half-draped over him. He heard her regular breathing indicating she was out.

No round two tonight? Never mind. You are a wild woman even drunk on your ass, Alexandra. I think I proved I can stand up to your other men tonight. You still might not believe I can replace them. But there's only enough room in your pussy for one dick, and I intend that it will be mine.

He fell asleep with a smile on his face.

Chapter Five

Alexandra was not used to having trouble concentrating when she was at work.

Damn him! Every fucking thing keeps reminding me of him and how good he is in bed! I've got to get my head back in the game!

She leaned forward and steepled her fingers together in the *I'm giving you my full attention* pose her father had taught her, but touching her fingers together made her inadvertently look at the fingers on the man who was sitting across the desk from her, explaining what he expected her to produce for his company, now that *his* father had convinced him she was the best in the business.

Look at those skinny little fingers. I'll bet he thinks he's got a big dick, but the women he's with know better. They ask him, "Is anything going on down there yet?"

She pursed her lips in a frown, so the smile wouldn't show.

Fingers...the first clue I had that my man mountain had a chubby choad that just won't stop! What a man! Good thing I'm woman enough to handle all he can dish out! Phew!

"Isn't that right, Alexandra?"

Shit! Shit! Shit! What the fuck is he asking me about?

She nodded at Bill, her VP of Marketing. He took that as her answer and pointed to the slide on the screen that was a part of his power point presentation. The new client asked him a question and she went back to remembering how good her weekend had been, ending with a perfect day yesterday.

Not only is he an animal in bed, but he's a fucking chef who works magic in the kitchen too. He let me sleep in so he could create a spectacular brunch. Then he brought in coffee and woke me up by licking and sucking me into being awake, then fucking me until I was screaming myself hoarse again!

Then we stayed naked and ate next to the balcony, enjoying the warm sunshine as we ate that eggy-cheesy thing he baked with potatoes and onions. He had fruit and mimosas ready for us too. After I ate until I couldn't move, we relaxed in the Jacuzzi, drinking more mimosas. Then we fucked in lots of my favorite positions until we passed out from pleasure. When we woke up later, he made some of the best steaks I've ever had, along with all of the side stuff I usually ignore. But he made them good too! If he keeps on feeding me like that I'm gonna gain a ton of weight. I'll have to work out extra-hard when I get home tonight.

She focused her eyes when the men in the room appeared to be finishing up their discussion. They got up and shook hands with each other. The new client approached her desk and extended his hand to her as well.

"You've got enough going on here that I think you can do what we need. I'll give you sixty days to get some results. If I'm not happy, I'll have to rethink my decision."

Alexandra gave him her most persuasive smile, the one she had used to get her dad to buy her anything she wanted... *like my first motorcycle.*

"We won't need that long to prove to you we can do what you want."

His eyebrows rose, while his eyes bored into her. "I hope so."

Once the door had closed behind him, Bill launched into his version of what had just happened. Alexandra forced herself to concentrate on his words.

And for a short time, she was able to keep her head in the game and ignore the persistent ache between her legs that reminded her she had done some vigorous and energetic fucking over the weekend.

* * * *

Tuesday afternoon Dmitri returned to the biker bar he'd been introduced to on Saturday night. He'd spent the past two days looking for some kind of employment.

If I'm gonna stick around and try to tame that redheaded wildcat, I'm gonna need a way to pay for shit and a place to stay. I wonder if Ivan knows anyone from around here.

He took a sip from the shot the bartender placed in front of him, then sent a text to Ivan. When he was done he looked up and watched idly as Joe, the bartender answered the phone.

"What? You know what it's like in here tonight! What the fuck do you mean you can't come in?"

As the person on the other end of the line spoke, the bartender's expression got angrier.

"I don't care how you're feeling. You just need to grow a pair and tell that bitch you're coming to work...yeah, I know she's got an itch only you can scratch."

Don't they all? Dmitri smiled.

"Then fuck you! Don't bother coming back; jag-off! Consider yourself fired!"

After slamming the phone down, the bartender strode angrily over to the small sink under the bar where Dmitri sat and splashed water everywhere as he took out his bad mood on the glasses.

"Trouble?" Dmitri asked as he watched the second broken glass being tossed into the garbage.

"Yeah. Son of a bitch who's been my bouncer on weeknights has got himself a new piece. Some young bimbo who keeps him up all night fucking her, then he's too damned tired to come to work. Asshole."

Dmitri looked around at the sparse crowd doing some late afternoon drinking.

"Don't look to me like that's gonna be a problem tonight."

"No? Tuesday night is darts contest night. By seven this place'll be packed. And once they all get good and tanked, they start accusing each other of cheating and the fighting starts. I don't know how the hell I'm gonna keep up with the drinks *and* collect the cover charge *and* keep the peace around here."

Dmitri leaned forward. "Are your bouncers allowed to have a few drinks while they work?"

Joe looked up quickly. "Why? You interested?"

"I might be."

He appraised Dmitri's size and seemed pleased with what he saw.

"You're the one came in with Alex on Saturday night, right? Hit one of her riders and knocked him unconscious without anyone seeing what you did?"

Dmitri nodded.

"Ten bucks an hour and all the vodka you can drink, as long as you keep everyone playing nice together. You can even order some food while you're working and it'll be part of your pay. I'll throw in ten percent of the cover charge if you stop any trouble before it gets out of hand. Deal?"

"Cash?"

Joe's eyes narrowed. "Why? You illegal?"

Unruffled, Dmitri smiled blandly. "Nah. I just hate having *the man* take a big chunk out of what I earn."

Joe nodded. "Okay, fine. Cash. Makes it easier for my accountant that way."

"Deal," Dmitri said as he shook the hand thrust in front of his face and turned to the door.

"I should go hang around by the main door, right?"

Joe poured another shot in his glass and nodded.

"Five bucks to come in, ten bucks if they're gonna play. I award cash prizes to the winning teams. Comes out of the take, so you're gonna need this."

He reached under the bar and pulled out a strong box with a key in the lock.

"You got it, boss." Dmitri grabbed the box and sauntered over to the door to settle down on the stool already there, putting the box onto a small table he found between the stool and the wall.

He sat on the stool, took a sip from his glass and looked around expectantly as he arranged his expression into a mean look to discourage challenges to his authority. *This is gonna be easy money.*

* * * *

Dmitri didn't hear his phone ringing over the noise of the jukebox and the yelling of the patrons, but he felt it vibrating in his pocket. He looked closely at it and saw it was after eleven, and that the fiery redhead was calling him. He smiled as he answered.

"Yeah?"

"Hello, Dmitri," she purred. "Miss me?"

"I'm hard already just hearing your voice...so yeah."

"And I've got my fingers in my pussy because I'm...hey! Why do I hear so much noise? Are you partying without me?"

"No, I..."

"Bullshit! I hear music and yelling and stuff. Where the hell are you?"

"I'm working."

"Where?"

"That bar you took me to on Saturday? I stopped here for a drink yesterday and they needed a weeknight bouncer. I got hired on the spot. Tonight's the billiards contest. Last night was darts. Tomorrow night's the wet tee-shirt contest with karaoke."

"Wet tee-shirt, huh? Think I could win?"

"Honey, if you put on a white T-shirt with no bra, I'd be fired for punching out all of the men who grabbed at your tits…or I'd be fired for fucking you on the pool table."

Alexandra was silent for so long that Dmitri asked, "You still there?"

He heard her moan and smiled.

"You just made yourself come, didn't you?"

"No, you made me come. I'm tempted to head down there right now in a white tee-shirt just to see what happens."

"Don't. So, why'd you call? I thought we were gonna stick to weekends only."

"Yeah, I know I told you that's my rule. I don't combine my biker-self with my businesswoman-self, but I can't stop thinking about you. My pussy has finally stopped aching from the pounding you gave me, but now I want some more."

Some guys walked in and Dmitri had to say, "Wait a minute, honey," while he collected their money and stamped the backs of their hands. Once he had put the money into the lock box he asked, "So what do you want from me?"

"Come over tonight."

"I'm not done until after one."

"I don't care. I'll wait up."

"Does that make this a booty call?"

"Yeah, but I'm the one who's calling, so you're the one supplying the booty."

"Whatever you say, babe."

"So are you coming or not?"

"Not yet, but I will be as soon as I can get there."

"I'd leave the door open but I know I don't have to. You just let yourself in and I'll be waiting for you."

"Keep it juicy until I get there."

"Bastard! I will."

He hung up and smiled at the phone.

How the hell am I going to convince such a horny woman that the only man she needs is me? She's used to getting what she wants from any man she asks. But playing hard-to-get is impossible. All I can think about is slamming myself into her again until she shrieks out my name. Damn!

* * * *

Shortly after one, Dmitri pushed the door closed and locked it. He listened for a moment and thought he heard a noise from the master bedroom, which was where he was headed anyway. He tossed his leather jacket onto the sofa and headed down the hall. What he saw when he got close to the open door made him stop in his tracks as all the blood in his body raced for his groin.

Alexandra was on her stomach on a weight bench, doing lateral flies. He only glanced for a quick moment at her back as the muscles bulged with each lift of the weights. His eyes grew larger, as did his cock, when he noticed she was wearing a white tee-shirt with a tiny, lacy white thong. Since she was lying on her stomach with her legs spread and her feet on either side of the bench, he had a great view of the area barely covered by the thong.

Holy fucking hell! Woman, you are trying to kill me!

The only noise he made was a strangled moan, but it was loud enough for Alexandra to put her weights down and sit up. She swung one leg around so that she reversed direction and what little ability Dmitri had to think left him. All he could do was stare lustfully at the thin white tee-shirt that accentuated her large, erect nipples, making even the bumps on her areolas harden under his gaze.

"Hi honey," she purred. "I did some cardio earlier, now I'm finishing up my weight-lifting. Gotta keep myself in shape so I can keep up with you, right?"

She licked her lips and smiled.

Dmitri gave up trying to speak. Instead he strode forward quickly, stopping directly in front of Alexandra. She turned her face up to stare into his eyes, while her hands began pushing her breasts together, then her fingers played with the nipples while Dmitri's eyes turned black with arousal.

The only noise in the room was his panting as he bent his head and captured one of her nipples in his mouth, sucking it though the tee-shirt. Alexandra sighed as she let him push her backwards to lie on the bench, his lips still attached to her, his teeth now nipping in between sweeps of his tongue. She closed her eyes to concentrate on the immensity of the feelings building in her, but opened them to moan in disappointment when he let go of her nipple with a *pop*.

His face doesn't even look human anymore! He looks like lust personified! Ooh, I have a feeling I'm gonna get it good tonight!

Dmitri put a large hand on either side of her ample hips and pulled her down to the edge of the bench before ripping of her thong by snapping the sides open. She watched as he feverishly tore at his pants, getting them open then not even bothering to step out of them. He grabbed her hips again and aimed himself at the inflamed, engorged mouth of her pussy, taking only a moment to rub himself around her opening, spreading their juices around before he pulled her up and stabbed his way into her in one forceful push.

He fills me! Every part of me is squeezing and he's wide enough to almost split me open when he pushes into me! I feel every ridge and vein on his cock!

"Oh, my fucking God! Deeper, Dmitri! Deeper!" Alexandra wrapped her legs around his hips and locked her ankles behind his ass. She looked up at his face as he worked. Sweat glistened on his face, set into a grimace of pleasure as he gritted his teeth trying to maintain control.

He let go of one hip while pulling out then pounded back into her again. He cupped a breast, pulling and rolling the nipple between his thumb and forefinger, his grip this side of pain. Alexandra began to wail as she felt her orgasm nearing. With a shriek that could wake the dead, she screamed out her pleasure, her eyelids squeezed tightly shut so she could watch the fireworks exploding in her head.

"Aah!" She took a quick breath. "Aah!"

Dmitri pushed in one final time and held her tightly against his groin as he exploded, his come spurting into her with the force of a geyser. He howled out his pleasure at the intensity of his orgasms as he came, riding along with Alexandra on the roller coaster of multiple orgasms, each of them dragging the other along with each new after-shock.

Countless long minutes passed as each of them panted from exertion, chests heaving with the need for oxygen to supply the blood still pounding through their bodies. Dmitri fell forward and Alexandra caught him before his hands stopped on the weight bench, his arms locked at the elbows, to keep the bulk of his weight from crushing her. She pressed her face to his chest, licking the salty sweat from his black chest hair, lightly teasing his nipples with her tongue. Her arms encircled his barrel of a chest, feeling him heave as his breathing gradually slowed down.

"And I thought I was done with the cardio part of my

work-out," she began when she could talk again.

Dmitri opened his eyes to stare into hers. Gradually a smile pulled the corners of his lips upwards.

"All I could think about after you called was what you would look like with a white tee-shirt on. And here you are. Do me a favor and don't ever wear it bra-less like this in public."

Alexandra tossed her hair to ask archly, "Oh? Why is that?"

"Because I'll have to kill any other man who tries to touch you, then I'll fuck you until you scream. I'm sorry, but it's not possible for me to react any other way. You make me crazy, like I'm not even human anymore..."

She smiled broadly. "Good! That's how you make me feel too."

"But now I need to sit down before my legs give out. They've finally stopped shaking, but with my pants still on my ankles, I can't maintain my balance for much longer."

She nodded. "I'll let you go for now, but once you get your pants completely off, you need to get into my bed for round two, you animal!"

His eyebrows rose. "Tomorrow's a workday for you, right? Means an early morning?"

Alexandra shrugged. "I don't care anymore. I spent the last two days at work remembering how much I love to fuck with you. I couldn't sit down without the aching from my pussy reminding me how wide you are, and how hard you push your way into me. Just thinking about it made me leak into a couple more slips and skirts that will now have to be dry-cleaned."

Dmitri smiled broadly while he threw his pants aside and held out his hands to pull her up and off of the bench. When she stood, he encircled her in his arms and crushed her to him fiercely, muttering into her hair, "I'm glad the memory burns in your mind. I've barely thought about anything else except how much I want to be inside of you, making you scream again. You are fast becoming an addiction for me, *Sashka*."

He felt her turn her head upwards to look at his face, so he relaxed his hold slightly. She gave his ass cheeks a final squeeze before her hands traveled up his back. They traced a lazy path up his stomach to his chest, to rest on his shoulders as she gazed into his eyes.

"What did you call me?"

"*Sashka*. It's a form of endearment in Russia for women named Alexandra."

Her eyebrows rose. "Oh, it is, huh? I had to read *The Brothers Karamazov* when I was in college. What drove me crazy was all the names each person had, depending on who was talking to them, and how closely-related they were. This is the same kind of thing, huh?"

Dmitri nodded slowly, his head lowering so he could brush his lips gently against hers.

"Yes, my woman," he breathed against her lips before trailing his tongue along the side of her chin down to her neck, where he blew into her ear and nipped her earlobe.

"*Your* woman? I don't *belong* to any man—" she began.

"Then let me convince you further that you belong wrapped around my cock."

With no apparent effort, he lifted her up and impaled her on his once-again rampant tool, holding her ass in his hands. She wrapped her legs around him, locking her ankles at his waist, and he walked across the room over to the bed. Once there he turned and sat backwards, still holding onto her ass while she ground herself against his pubic bone. This time Alexandra pushed him backwards to lie down on her bed with his knees bent and his feet still on the floor. She rode him hard for a while before pulling herself up and off of him.

"Move back up on the bed," she demanded. "I need to get better traction. I need you to raise your knees up behind me."

"Your wish is my command, my queen," Dmitri intoned solemnly, doing as she requested and moving up onto the middle of the huge bed.

Alexandra crawled over to cover his groin with hers.

* * * *

They both passed out from sheer exhaustion later in the night. When Alexandra arrived at her office much later than her usual time in the morning, she offered no excuse. No one commented on her tardiness to her face for a number of reasons. First she was the owner's daughter and their boss, the one who signed their paychecks. Secondly, her belligerent attitude didn't allow for anyone to comment on her personal business. And third, her difficulty with both walking and sitting comfortably was just too obvious.

The women who realized the reason for her discomfort were shocked while the men were jealous that someone was obviously enjoying the side of her she never showed at the office.

She cracked the whip and everyone was suddenly twice as industrious as they were before her arrival.

Chapter Six

On Friday afternoon Dmitri picked up the ingredients for a stew dinner and made himself at home in her kitchen. He thought she would have been home sooner, but as it was he had the time to get everything assembled and into the oven by the time he heard the front door open.

He walked out into the living room wearing only the apron, which jutted out in front where his cock was demonstrating how happy it was that she was finally home.

"Are you always this late on a Friday?" He asked as she walked up to him and he enfolded her in his arms for a bear hug.

She spoke while her hands explored his naked ass, and she bit his neck gently.

"No. I had to attend a baby shower for one of the secretaries. I've never been so bored in my life! I mean, I know fucking can result in a baby, but the way I see it, sex is so much more fun when it's done just for recreation."

Dmitri's lips twitched in amusement at the look on her face.

"Why'd you go then?"

Alexandra sighed. "Because it's expected of me because I've got a snatch. If I was a man, they'd let me off. But since I'm not, I had to attend. I left while the preggo was still opening gifts, but after she'd opened my envelope with the check in it. I never know what the fuck to get, so I just give a chunk of money so she can buy whatever she needs."

"I'm guessing you're not the kind of woman who dreams of having a baby?"

Alexandra barked out a harsh laugh.

"You got that right! Getting knocked up means some man thinks he owns your body just because his sperm is doing some construction in there. Then he expects you to fuck only him because he wants more of them...the asshole. From what I've heard from my sister, childbirth is something I'd like to avoid at all costs. Men like lots of kids because they don't have to have them."

Dmitri shrugged. "I'd like a few...someday."

"Don't look at me when you say that!"

"You don't ever want to settle down?"

"And give up my other men? For what? Boring vanilla sex with some guy who won't even go down on me anymore because he thinks he doesn't have to, but who expects blow-jobs whenever he demands them? Fuck no!"

"Men usually say it's the women who won't blow them anymore, once they have a ring on their finger."

Alexandra's eyebrows rose. "Oh? I love to suck cock. I don't plan on ever stopping that, since it gets me so hot. But I also love smearing my cream all over a man's face."

"What if the man who knocks you up doesn't do vanilla?"

"Will he still let me do other men?"

"Fuck no."

"Then no thanks. Besides, I've got my business to run. Dad trained me to do it all along, because Mom couldn't have any more kids after my sister was born. I was the oldest, so I'm the one who keeps his life's work running. He's already got a couple of grandchildren from her, and she's probably gonna pop a couple more out before she's too old. So that leaves me free to do whatever I want."

She smiled at the look on Dmitri's face. "But don't worry. I won't hold it against you that you want kids. You'll probably want to look for a younger woman to do that with anyway. I'll just keep my IUD in place and we'll both be happy that way. How's that?"

His eyes burned into hers for a long moment, then he shrugged.

"Fine."

Alexandra sniffed at the air. "So what's cooking? It smells really good in here, like someone who knows what they're doing has been making use of the kitchen. All I use it for is the fridge to keep my beer cold."

Dmitri began to unbutton her blouse. "Stew. It'll need to cook for a couple of hours. We'll have to find some way to amuse ourselves until we can eat...maybe working up an appetite somehow?"

Alexandra reached up behind his neck and untied the apron, then pulled it off and threw it to the side. She ran her hands all over his skin, pulling gently at the long, black chest hair and tweaking at his nipples while he pushed her blouse off of her shoulders.

Her white lace bra didn't cover her up as much as it enticed him, letting him see the large reddish-brown nipples already hardening under his gaze. When he touched them they leapt into his palms with delight.

"I feel like I disappointed you somehow," Alexandra said as their hands reacquainted themselves with each other's bodies.

"It's not possible for you to disappoint me," Dmitri murmured. "I have no expectations. I enjoy every part of you that you are willing to share with me."

Suddenly Alexandra sank to her knees. One hand circled behind to Dmitri's ass, so she could squeeze his cheeks together and massage them. The other hand roamed all over his cock, before it settled at the base. Her thumb and forefinger held him tightly while her fingers played with his sac, fondling his balls and rolling them against each other.

Dmitri bit his lip as her tongue began to lap at him, long, cat-like strokes from the ball sac up to the tip, where she spread the fluids leaking out of him all over the head. She kept on licking up his length until his legs were shaking from the effort of holding himself upright. Then she covered his wide head with her lips and began to suck him into her mouth. He groaned.

Once she had him in her mouth, Alexandra moved to allow herself a better angle, and she began to move her head up and down, trying to swallow what barely fit into her mouth.

Holy shit! Is that the back of her throat? Is this wild woman managing to swallow my cock? Sweet Jesus! She is! I can feel her throat muscles all around me. Oh, my God!

Dmitri groaned again, this time in ecstasy. Alexandra continued to bob her head, swallowing him on the down-strokes, licking along the length of him on the way back up. She fought hard against her gag reflex, and enjoyed knowing Dmitri was helpless against the pleasure her mouth was giving to his cock.

She knew even before he did when he was close to losing control. Her movements got quicker and shallower. Suddenly he froze and she used both hands to supplement her mouth. With a howl worthy of a beast, he exploded. She pulled back and milked him with her hands, licking at the ropes of sticky fluid that spurted out of him like lava from a volcano.

She held onto him then, her head pressed against his belly, her arms encircling his waist. She felt his legs trembling as his body rode out the aftershocks while still remaining upright. His hands wrapped themselves in her hair and she ignored the pain as even his hands shook, pulling at the long curls of her mane. They remained that way for a few long moments, while Dmitri recovered enough to remember how to speak again.

"Is it my turn for an appetizer?" he asked in a gruff voice, harsh from passion.

Alexandra looked up at his face and smiled.

"Let's get me naked too. Then we can work up a real appetite!"

That's just what they did.

* * * *

They finally showered and dressed sometime in the late afternoon on Saturday. Once Alexandra had put on her biker leather, her personality changed again. Dmitri smiled as he saw her hardening around the edges.

"You're a strong independent woman when you're *Alex Business Owner*. But once you turn into *Alex Biker Queen*, you're all hard bitch."

Alexandra nodded. "You got that right. No soft edges on this female. I'm as hard as the cocks of the men I fuck. No one pushes me around."

He watched her ass move as she walked to the door then turned to give him a come-hither look.

"Coming, mister?"

"Yes, ma'am," he answered as he strode across the room to follow her out the door.

Once again they had to take the SUV, since snow had fallen during the day. Alexandra drove, but handed her keys to Dmitri once they got to the bar.

Noticing his raised eyebrows, she smiled.

"This way you won't have to fight me for them when I'm tanked."

"You trust my driving more than your own?"

She nodded. "When I'm drinking...yeah. Just get me home

in one piece and we can fuck like animals again." She patted the side of his face.

Dmitri nodded. "Yes, boss."

Her lips curled up as she met his eye right before she pushed the door open to stride purposefully into the crowded, noisy bar.

Her gang was already there again, so she was greeted loudly by all of them as she made her way over to the bar to grab the beer the bartender had poured for her as she approached. Dmitri took the shot of vodka already poured for him also and followed her to the tables. He spent the next few hours watching her closely as she talked, laughed, shot pool, and flirted with any man who caught her eye.

He was toying with getting up to challenge a biker who was tongue-kissing Alexandra and playing with her ass, when he remembered he was the weeknight bouncer for the place, and it wouldn't be good for his employment if he was to start a fight. He patted the keys to her car in his pocket and smiled, taking another sip from his glass.

He looked up briefly to nod in acknowledgement when one of the men in her gang sat down at his table. The man was tall and built like a football player, with an unshaven face that was supposed to make him look tough. Since it wasn't yet a beard, it just looked unkempt.

I think his name is Rich, Dmitri thought, trying to remember the names of the men he had been introduced to already. *The vibe I'm getting from him is definitely hostile. What's his problem?*

There was a lot of noise from the jukebox and the crowd in the bar, but he heard what the man said even though it was said in a low tone.

"Enjoy it while you can, dude."

"What?"

"Having her favorite cock. We've all had our turn being her favorite. Then the next guy she fucks turns into her new favorite. You get used to it after a while."

Dmitri regarded him solemnly. "I won't."

The other man smiled with his lips, but his eyes looked bitter. "Yes, you will. Once it gets to be riding weather, we'll all head out to her place near Mille Lacs for long weekends. She's got a playroom built in the barn. That's where you'll learn to share."

"Playroom?"

The other man nodded. "Yeah. Manacles built into the wall. Whips. Handcuffs. Dildos and cock rings. Ben-wa balls. All of that shit. If it can be used for great sex, it's there. That's when you'll realize that if you can't have her to yourself, at least you can still have her."

Dmitri turned away from the man to watch the red-haired vixen of his dreams continue to drink and flirt with other men. He felt himself beginning to growl from a place deep in his throat.

The other man laughed. "You'll see. It's better than nothing." He got unsteadily to his feet, swayed for a moment, then made his way back to the bar for another beer.

Dmitri continued to watch the woman closely.

Should I go make her pay attention to me? For what? To start a fight? With him or with her? I'm gonna be the one fucking her tonight, so what would be the point?

His view was impeded by the swaying hips of a short woman with long black hair who approached him meaningfully.

"Hi, you big stud. I'm Angela. I ride with José. Wanna dance?"

"Who's José?"

She nodded her head towards the pool table.

"He's the one feeling up the queen right now. So I've got no one to dance with. I just put some money into the box for Santana and listen...it's starting. Dance with me to *me ritmo* of *Oye Como Va*."

Dmitri smiled as he joined her on the small, crowded space that passed for a dance floor and they began to do a sexy cha-cha.

The rest of the night passed in the same way. Dmitri kept an eye on the red-haired woman, while other men kept putting their hands on her. He repeatedly had to stop himself from interfering with what was obviously her usual way of entertaining herself and letting loose after her tough work-week.

After enough shots of vodka, Dmitri realized a line had been crossed when he saw a hand disappearing down the back of Alexandra's jeans. He'd been a patient man, but enough was enough! He got up from his chair and purposefully made his way over to the dance floor to cut in on his queen.

"My turn," he said gruffly to the man who had been groping Alexandra while they danced. It was Rich, the same man who had spoken to him earlier.

"Dmitri," Alexandra drawled at him, slightly slurring her words, her eyes glassy and unfocused. "I was wondering when you would come to claim me."

His hands held her ass while he pulled her closer, his hard cock rubbing against her belly as they swayed to the music.

"You were mine when we walked in the door. You'll be mine when we leave...and it's time for us to leave. Now."

Alexandra nodded and smiled. "So we can go fuck like rabbits?"

He nodded. "Yeah."

Alexandra pushed away from him and turned in a circle, waving lazily around at everyone in her general vicinity.

"G'night everyone. I've got some important fucking to do. See ya's all next week. Call me if the snow has cleared enough for bikes." She turned to Dmitri with a smile. "Let's go, big guy. My pussy's dripping just for you."

Yeah, after half of the men in your gang felt you up, getting you ready for a good fucking. I'm drunk enough to let you know how that made me feel. Once we get back to your place, your ass is mine!

The drive back didn't take long. Once they were back in her condo, Alexandra peeled her clothing off as she walked to the bathroom. Dmitri used the guest bathroom and was lying on her bed waiting for her when she got into the bedroom.

Alexandra climbed onto the bed and he pulled her into his arms. She wrapped a leg around his hip and ground herself against him. He obliged by pushing his hips forward to slide himself into her, since she was already so slippery that it was easier than usual. When he pulled out right before she came, she pouted.

"Hey! What's up with you? I was so close!"

Dmitri nodded. "Yeah, I know. But you made me jealous tonight. I had to watch while other men felt you up, and I knew I couldn't stop them because you wanted them to do it. You were testing me to see what I could take. Now, I'm gonna see how much you can take."

She grinned back at him, her eyes glassy and bright.

"Am I gonna like it?"

"Uh-huh. Eventually."

Dmitri pushed Alexandra up so she was closer to the head of the bed. He pushed her arms up and quickly tied each wrist using scarves he had found in her drawers.

Alexandra looked back and forth and smiled. "Kinky!"

Dmitri crawled down to the bottom of the mattress and tied each ankle using the longer scarves he'd attached under the bed. When he was done, he stood to admire his work.

Alexandra began to pull on the scarves and appeared dismayed that she was unable to move her arms and legs very far.

"C'mon, Dmitri. You got me tied up good and tight. What're you gonna do with me now?"

Dmitri spent the next few hours indulging himself. He'd lick and suck at every part of Alexandra's body, then he'd poke himself into her and fuck her hard. Just when she'd start to moan, or her body would let him know she was getting close to coming, he'd pull out and get up from the bed. He'd go out of the room to use the bathroom, or to get another drink. Sometimes he'd get himself a snack. Then when he got back, he'd ignore her alternately swearing at him, then pleading with him to let her come. He'd watch her for a while as she pulled at the scarves trying to free herself, then he'd make sure she was watching while he stroked himself hard again.

Sometimes he'd straddle her head and push himself into her mouth, choking her with the ferocity of his strokes, since she didn't have any hands free to control his movements. He'd pull back before he came and torture her with licking and sucking for some time, then he'd fuck her hard again just to the point of orgasm. Then he'd get up and leave the room again.

By the time the sun was beginning to come up, Alexandra was done with swearing at him. She was reduced to sobbing while she begged him to let her come. The alcohol had worn off and she was exhausted. Dmitri had an evil grin on his face as he lifted her ass up and slid a pillow underneath her, to allow for deeper penetration.

He leaned forward and pushed her breasts together, trying to suck on both of her large nipples at the same time as he pushed his hips forward and buried himself deeply into her core. When he felt himself pushing against her cervix while his balls draped on her ass, he knew he was as far in as it was possible for him to be. He began a rhythm he knew he wouldn't be able to keep up for long. He was already so overdue for an orgasm himself that the pressure in his lower spine became an insistent ache that demanded release.

This time he allowed the pressure to determine the speed

and depth. He gripped her hips tightly as he pounded himself into her, grunting out his feelings.

"No one else can touch you! You're *my* woman! Your cunt belongs to me! Every part of you is mine! Tell me! Tell me, you hot, horny bitch! Who gets to fuck you?"

Alexandra was almost delirious with pleasure. She whimpered her answers.

"You do! You are my man! Your cock owns me! Fuck me harder! Harder! Hard...aah!"

She shrieked like a banshee while she came, twisting and pulling at the bonds that tied her up, gnashing her teeth and screaming, her face set in a rictus of agony-based ecstasy. Her body shook and trembled as every cell in her body exploded. Dmitri finally gave up his control and rode along with her on the cascade of multiple orgasms that made them both pass out because their bodies couldn't take being conscious anymore.

A short while later, Dmitri twitched awake as every muscle in his body relaxed into sleep mode. He realized Alex was still tied up and he carefully undid the knots. He momentarily felt guilt at the red marks on her wrists and ankles. But when he got back into bed next to her and pulled her close into his arms again, she sighed with contentment and snuggled into his skin.

He closed his eyes and joined her in the deep dreamless sleep of a totally sexually satiated state of exhaustion.

Chapter Seven

The next few weeks passed by, with a routine becoming established. It was still too early in spring for the snow to be gone, so very few were brave or foolish enough to ride their Harleys. Not only were they temperamental machines that didn't perform well in extreme cold, they were so expensive that few were willing to have their bikes exposed to the salt and sand strewn about on the icy roads to help with traction.

Dmitri had found a small, furnished efficiency apartment, and paid cash on a month-by-month basis. He was sleeping over at Alexandra's expensive condo four nights a week, so he figured that for three nights a week he could stand being cramped. Plus when he looked around he laughed to himself, remembering what life had been like in Moscow.

This would have been a very expensive apartment there! Especially with real furniture... not an egg crate in sight. And the appliances even work. Only in America! I am a rich man!

As it turned out, Ivan did indeed know *some people* in Minneapolis-St. Paul who had occasional uses for the talents Dmitri had been taught by his family so he could be useful in the *business*.

There are always people who don't want to pay their debts, and who need to be persuaded that paying is better than not paying. As long as no one is asking me to seriously hurt or kill anyone, I'm good. I don't want to have to leave town. I have a reason to be here, and I'm not ready to admit defeat yet.

He had expected Alexandra to be angry with him for torturing her that Saturday night. Instead, she seemed to regard him with new respect. He was greatly amused to notice the next few Saturday nights, that while she still flirted with other men, and even groped a few, she didn't seem to be paying attention to the man who was groping her at that moment as much as she was watching him for his reactions.

He quickly realized that when his face reflected she was going too far, she would roll her hips as she walked over to where he was, and would sit on him and perform a lap-dance worthy of a professional. Or she would pull him up and insist it was time for him to take her home.

Fridays, Sundays and even Wednesdays were nights for great sex…especially when she was enthusiastic about the food he was enjoying cooking for her. But Saturday night sex was explosive, even approaching violent. Alexandra enjoyed provoking Dmitri to have to assert his right to her, and she made him prove over and over again that he was man enough to be her equal…and to dominate her when she let him.

Which is why he was so perplexed when she told him on a Wednesday night after a few weeks had passed predictably, that she wasn't going to be able to go with him on Saturday night to the biker bar.

"And why not?" He asked her as they were soaking in her Jacuzzi, enjoying their after-dinner drunken coffees.

"Because every year my Dad's Country Club has this charity ball thing. He made me a member years ago, because the only way to be admitted is to be sponsored in by an active member of good standing. He wanted me to be a member in my own right, to represent his company there. I don't golf worth a shit, so I rarely go there unless he insists, and then I only stay as long as I have to, and I duck out as soon as I can."

"No pool tables there?" Dmitri teased, since she often cleaned up the table, treating anyone she played against to the sight of her bending over the table wearing tiny denim shorts that rode up the crack of her ass. Or if they were facing her, they'd have to deal with the sight of her huge breasts hanging down like some kind of luscious fruit ripe for the plucking, while she'd sink every ball on the table, including the eight ball, and make her opponent pay up. Dmitri had only played her a few times, and even he couldn't keep his mind on the game when all of the blood in his body kept racing to his groin as his dick asked him, *Did you see that? Holy shit, did you see that? Gimme that now!*

Alexandra took a sip of her coffee and sighed, "Well, there are tables there, but with the way I have to be dressed when I'm there, I can't relax and enjoy myself."

Dmitri chuckled. "I should go with you there. Maybe I could even pay attention to the game long enough to beat you."

Alexandra stuck out her tongue at him.

"No, I don't think you'd fit in there. You're not their kind of person."

Dmitri's eyebrows rose. "Oh? What kind of person is that?"

Alexandra shrugged. "You know. The old-money kind of people. The men who look like they were born wearing a business suit. The only time they don't wear a tie is on the golf course, and their choice of what to wear out there is so hideous you almost want to beg them to put that damned tie back on. They bring women with them who are trophy wives, since they long ago divorced the woman who worked two jobs to help them get their degrees, or to get their business established. That's how you end up with so many old men with young children, and young wives who are barely older than their kids from their previous marriages."

"You don't sound like you approve of these people, so why do you go there?"

"I told you, my Dad is a member. He used to do a lot of business out on the golf course back when drinking was encouraged on so many of the holes they'd have temporary bars set up on many of them. He's still pissed at me for not taking to golf the way he expected me to. I told him I'll run the business, and I'll join him there when required to, but I refuse to put on ugly Bermuda shorts and polo shirts to whack small balls around on over-manicured grass that smells weird from all of the chemicals they dump on it."

Dmitri asked a question he'd long been wanting to. "Does your Dad have any idea what you do with your weekends?"

Alexandra leaned back and laughed, shaking her head.

"Hell no! He knows I ride my Harley, since he bought me my first one when I was still in college. He has no fucking idea I'm the queen of my gang, or that I even *have* a gang! I want to keep it that way. I work hard to keep my *weekday me* and my *weekend me* separate."

"That must be difficult for you to do when your worlds overlap, like this Saturday night," Dmitri observed.

"As long as I don't drink too much when I'm at the Club, I'm okay. It used to be harder for me when I was younger and didn't have much control over myself when I was getting tanked. Now I know enough to stick with something I don't like enough to drink much of it, like white wine. That way I look like everyone else, but I won't drink so much that I actually tell any of them what I really think of them and their lame-ass Club!"

"So, what happens at this Charity Ball?"

Alexandra took another drink then slid further down under the water and sighed.

"Oh, the usual stuff...nothing interesting. There's a silent auction to raise money. There're appetizers and drinks before dinner. Then a meal that's barely edible...especially compared to what you've been spoiling me with lately!"

Dmitri reached forward to clink his coffee mug against hers, and she blew him a kiss.

"Speaking of that, what's in this drunken coffee that's so good?"

"The recipe changes based on what I have available. This time there's Kahlua, Amaretto, and Baileys. I'm glad you like it."

"I like everything you make for me to eat or drink."

"What else happens at the charity event after you eat dinner?"

"There's dancing and more drinking after the meal. I usually cut out as soon after dinner as I can manage."

"Will you be your Dad's date?"

She grinned. "Hell no! He's got his trophy wife for that. I just go stag. Then he spends a lot of time introducing me to any single men he's met there in the past year, trying to set me up. He has no idea what I'm like, or why all of the guys there are so fucking unsuitable for me."

Dmitri laughed. "Yeah, you'd probably chew them up and spit them out as used-up husks barely resembling the men they used to be."

"You got that right! There's no real men there...not like you."

Dmitri's eyes narrowed. "But you won't take me with you there?"

Alexandra shook her head. "No! You're not like them...."

Dmitri's voice held a hint of danger. "You don't think I could fit in?"

She gave him a sharp look then, when he smiled at her, she convinced herself she was imagining things.

"No, and I'm glad of it. I wouldn't ever let any of those dickless wimps into my bed. But you? You're welcome any time you want to be here."

Dmitri put his mug down on the side of the Jacuzzi and leaned forward to wrap his hands around her breasts, floating on the surface of the water. Both nipples hardened in his palms as he began to knead and fondle the rest of her softness.

"Speaking of being in your bed..." he began in a low growl.

"Yeah, I'm waterlogged enough for now," Alexandra replied as she stood up, water cascading off of her skin, enjoying his lustful gaze as she grabbed for a towel and put one foot on the side of the Jacuzzi to begin drying her legs off.

Dmitri got up on his knees and moved closer to her, his face at just the right height for him to use his tongue to lap at her folds. He used both of his hands to spread her labia while his thumbs massaged the seams inside the inner lips. He continued to assault her senses, as his teeth lightly grazed her clit, biting it gently, before he went back to lapping at the juices flowing out of her for him.

Suddenly Alexandra stiffened and moaned, as she reached forward to press his head tighter against her swollen mons. As she came, fluids erupted out of her, and Dmitri lapped at all of them.

"Mmmm," he hummed against her pubic bone. "Come for me, my *Sashka*."

When her legs began to shake he stood up and picked her up, impaling her on his cock and stepping out of the tub with her attached to him. She wrapped her arms around his shoulders and crossed her ankles against his ass. He ignored the towels and strode out into the bedroom. When he reached the bed he felt it with his knees first, because his eyes were closed to better enjoy the feeling of having her impaled on his cock while he walked.

Dmitri fell forward and when Alexandra hit the bed, his weight forced him so deeply into her, she grunted with the impact. Then they both began to move and the next few hours were spent in luxuriously fucking in every position they could think of to enjoy each other. When Alexandra fell asleep first, Dmitri held her closely in his arms, enjoying the feel of her skin against his, while he began to plan his next move in *Operation: Tame the Red-haired Wildcat*.

Chapter Eight

I didn't think it was possible for this to get even more boring than it's been, year after fucking year! But it has.

Alexandra stood alone, off to one side in the huge greatroom where drinks and appetizers were served before dinner. She shifted from one foot to the other, her feet begging for relief from the spiked heels she wore to accentuate her long legs.

Her dress was conservative by most standards, made from an olive green silk blend with thin spaghetti straps that dug into her shoulders while they strained to hold up her breasts. The dress draped in the front, but no amount of fabric could conceal the cleavage that had always drawn leers from the men and jealous glances from the women, even at society events like this one. Some of her tattoos were covered by the fabric, and the few that showed were colorful butterflies and flowers in colors that complemented her dress. She hated having to dress to please others instead of herself, especially on a weekend night. She sighed with annoyance at nothing in particular and everything in general.

She looked around in dismay at the usual crowd of older men wearing tailored power suits with accessories that screamed out *disposable wealth!* The women were all wearing expensive jewelry with their revealing gowns designed to show off their salon-tanned and toned bodies.

Hmm, wonder how many hours she spends at the gym getting her arms that thin? Too bad she can't do anything about her bony ass. And those implants of hers? Honey, these girls are real...yours look like they're gonna explode any minute. Judging by the amount of silicon that must be in them we'll all have to run for cover!

To cover up her smile, she took another sip from her glass of Riesling and snuck a quick look at her watch.

I wonder if Dmitri is already at the bar. He told me he wouldn't miss me too much, since the other females in my gang will be there. I wonder which one of them he'll go home with. And why should I care? I don't wanna be tied down to just him...so he's gotta be free to fuck other women too, right? But if he does, should I make him start using a condom? Or should I figure that as long as it's one of my friends, she's clean? But if it's not someone I know? Then what? And how will I know?

Alexandra was so busy with her thoughts she didn't hear her Father approaching her from behind. When he cleared his throat she turned and almost swallowed her tongue.

"Alex, I've been looking for you all over! I know you don't like when I introduce you to men not directly in our business, but this man here represents a conglomerate of interests from Russia. They aren't big in the US market yet, but if they ever get to the point where they need our expertise, it would be nice if we knew we would be in the running at least for an interview. Isn't that right, Dmitri?"

Dmitri wore a European-styled power suit so tailored to him it had to be hand-made. It flawlessly hugged every part of his body, accentuating his broad shoulders and tapered waist. The trousers had generous pleats in the front for a smoother line, amply covering up what Alexandra knew was under them, making her mouth go dry as she forced herself to not stare. His shoes looked to be hand-tooled Italian leather Oxfords, and his conservative tie was held in place by a tack with a diamond encrusted on it. As he held out his hand to shake hers, Alexandra idly noticed the cuff links on his sleeves had the same diamonds on them as his tie tack. The overall impression she got from looking at him was this was a man born to wealth, who only walked among the plebeians when he had to; otherwise he stayed on Mount Olympus, within his own social group.

She tried to speak, but had no voice. She cleared her throat and tried again, her hand still held in Dmitri's massive paw as both men waited patiently for her to acknowledge him.

"I'm please to meet you, mister..." she began then turned to her dad, her hand still being held. "What did you say his name was?"

"Dmitri Illyanovich." Her father smiled at the man. "I did pronounce it right, didn't I?"

For Dad to be so ingratiating, he's totally under Dmitri's spell! Either that, or I've been played for a fool in a major way. What the fuck?

Alexandra felt her face begin to hurt as the fake smile she wore caused muscle fatigue. Her eyes searched Dmitri's face but he kept up the act of never having met her before.

"This is your lovely daughter who runs your company, Mister Blackstone? You are indeed a lucky man, to have produced such beauty. Yet for her to be as intelligent as the head of your firm is known to be, must be a source of inordinate pride for you."

Dmitri bent his head down to kiss the back of her hand. "I'm honored to meet you, Miss Blackstone. I hope that in the future I can become important enough to merit some of your attention."

Feeling her father's eyes on her, she bit back her sarcastic responses and replied in a tone she hoped was neutral. "I hope so also. Father so rarely introduces me to men who can present me with an interesting challenge..." she hesitated a split second before continuing, "...in the workplace."

While they stared at each other, Alexandra's father glanced across the room to announce, "Ah, I see my wife is signaling to me from the entrance to the dining room. Would you consider joining us at our table, Mister Illyanovich?"

Without taking his eyes away from the stare-down with Alexandra, Dmitri replied smoothly, "If there is room at your table for one more diner, I'd be honored to join you tonight."

He turned to smile at the senior Blackstone. "And please, call me Dmitri."

"Excellent! And you can call me Thomas. I'll tell my wife we need to save two seats. Come join us when you're ready."

Dmitri watched as Thomas strode across the room back to his wife and bent low to talk directly into her ear. She glanced across the room at them and nodded before they walked with her hand on his arm, into the dining room.

Alexandra had enough. She turned quickly and walked out through the doors left unlocked for smokers to seek refuge on the balcony. She didn't stop until she had reached the opposite end of it and leaned against the ornate railing.

Dmitri followed her closely and, as she contemplated whether or not she would break a leg if she jumped, he spoke into her ear. His lips were so close to her skin the hairs on her neck stood at attention and a shiver ran down her spine before taking a detour to send the tingling sensation to the juncture between her thighs, making her legs shake.

"You don't appear to be happy to see me, *Sashka*."

She whirled around to face him. "What the fuck are you doing here? How did you even find the right place? This is an invitation-only event. What the hell kind of conglomerate are you supposed to represent? And how did you pick my dad out of the crowd, to get him to introduce you to me?"

Dmitri smiled at her, shaking his head. "You don't really want to know the answers to all of those questions. The only question you really want to know is why I'm here. The answer should be obvious. I'm here because it's Saturday night and you're here. Where else would I be?"

Sparks flew out of her eyes as she spat out, "At the bar? Fucking one of the biker babes there? Not here, intruding on my private life!"

He didn't back off, but stared into her eyes. "Private life? Is there anything more private than what you and I have shared for weeks now?"

"Okay, my weekday life. My businesswoman persona. You're not a part of this part of my life. You don't belong here."

A smile played with the corners of his mouth. "But that's where you are so wrong, *Sashka*. I belong wherever you are. I told you when I met you we both wear many faces and many names. I actually told your father my real name, though your knowing that gives you more power over me than I had intended for you to have at this point. But it will make things easier to explain to him when we tell him we're going to be married."

"*What*," she shrieked as her face registered anger and shock.

"Oh, did I say that out-loud? My bad. We'd better get into the dining room or your father and his lovely trophy wife will wonder where we are, since we'll be missing the soup course."

"Of all of the delusional, conceited, over-bearing..."

"Yes, yes, we can argue later. I don't know about you, but I'm hungry."

He reached out and took hold of her elbow and began walking towards the unlocked door back into the brightly-lit great room.

She walked without thinking about what she was doing, as her mind continued to try to process what was going on.

"But..." she sputtered as the door shut behind them.

"Later, Alexandra, we don't want your father to suspect we

have already met, do we? That might lead to some embarrassing questions."

He glanced over at her and smiled. She glared at him as they were ushered by the wait-staff into the dining room. A quick look around the room led them to the table her father was seated at, as he stood up and waved to get their attention.

"There you are, you two. Where did you go?"

"Your beautiful daughter wanted to show me the view of the golf course from the balcony. She also explained the national presence that a company of your size and stature could offer to my partners, should we decide we need help in introducing our products to your market."

Thomas wasn't sure what to make of his daughter's face, but he definitely approved of her continuing to demonstrate for their new acquaintance why the company he had built from scratch was so formidable. So he pointed to the two chairs he had saved opposite him from his wife, and he introduced Dmitri to the people seated at their table. As the soup was being served, he made sure Dmitri's glass was full of wine and launched into a discussion of international relations as they pertained to marketing and sales.

While he noticed his daughter wasn't her usual talkative self, he put that down to her working such long hours for the firm that hired them on a contingency basis. And besides, Dmitri had many interesting observations that at least the men at the table found fascinating as he compared the marketing environment of the Communist and pre-Glasnost USSR with the recent developments in Russia.

Alexandra watched surreptitiously as they were served each course, and noticed that not only were Dmitri's manners impeccable, but he ate in the European style, holding his knife in his right hand, and his fork in his left, instead of just cutting his food that way, then putting the knife down to eat with his right hand, as was the custom in the US. She realized with annoyance he was more cultured and sophisticated than she was, having traveled on many of the continents, while she was *an all-American gal*. If any of the women at the table excused themselves to leave for the powder room, Dmitri would stand up in deference and respect, then seat himself slowly back down, without missing a beat of the conversation he was involved in. She didn't really taste most of what she ate, but she drank more wine than she intended to, even though it wasn't her first choice of what to drink with a beef dinner.

Once the dinner plates were removed and coffee served, the conversation became centered on what the chef, who was known for his desserts, might have created for them that night. Alexandra was only half paying attention when she almost jumped up in alarm as she felt something rubbing her right thigh. She looked on the table and saw Dmitri drinking his coffee with his right hand, and realized it must be his left hand that was now actively caressing her upper thigh under the tablecloth.

Dmitri turned to her to smile in a casual manner and asked, "So tell me, Miss Blackstone, will the weather ever get warmer here in Minneapolis? Or was I lied to, and the only temperature ever recorded up here is cold, cold, and colder? It is uncomfortably close to what I've experienced in Siberia and hoped to have left behind me."

Alexandra tried for a natural smile, but his hand was insistently rubbing between her thighs. She tried to stop him by squeezing them closely together, but that only exacerbated the problem, since now not only were her thighs pressing on her clit, but Dmitri's magic fingers had been captured also, and were continuing to stimulate her in ways she couldn't allow with her Dad sitting on the other side of the offender.

"Um, we do get to spring eventually, usually by Mother's Day in mid-May. Certainly by Memorial Day. Then a few weeks later summer arrives, and the good times roll until fall hits in September and the snow returns by October."

He nodded. "So you have…what…three or four months out of the year that you can enjoy outdoor activities? Like driving a convertible or riding a Harley?"

Now he's gone too far! Groping me and taunting me about my bike here, of all places. I'll show him!

She began to push herself away from the table abruptly, and his fingers had to stop what they were doing before they were revealed.

"If you'll excuse me, I need to visit the powder room. And please let the server know I'm not interested in any dessert."

"May I have yours?" Dmitri asked with a wicked smile playing on his lips as he rose in respect for her being up. "I have an incessant desire for sweet things on my tongue."

"Suit yourself," she said tartly as she headed for the exit to the hall.

Once in the bathroom Alexandra spent an inordinate time on her appearance, even though she carried only lipstick in her bag. She pretended to be adjusting her dress and fussing with her make-up, to put off having to head back out to the surreal dilemma she'd been presented with. Eventually she sighed heavily and pushed the door open. Since there wasn't any sign of Dmitri, she quickly hurried over to the bar in the great-room. The lighting had been lowered for the evening, and the DJ was putting the finishing touches on his equipment.

She approached the bartender who was putting out napkins to get ready for the incipient crowd.

"Do you have Jack Daniels?"

"No, Ma'am."

"What kind of whiskey do you have?"

"Name-brands?"

She nodded wordlessly.

He began to list the choices but she soon stopped him.

"Give me a double shot of Maker's Mark."

He turned to fill her order and she felt movement behind her and knew without turning around that Dmitri had found her.

"Isn't that kind of strong when you're trying to maintain your image in front of all of these people?"

She hissed at him. "Leave me alone!"

He chuckled in her ear. "I can't do that, *Sashka*. You're in my blood. You're becoming a part of me."

She whirled on him. "That can't continue!"

"Are you ready for it to end?"

She stared into his dark eyes for a long moment. When the bartender returned with her glass, Dmitri turned to him. "Do you have Beluga vodka?"

A slow smile spread across the man's face. "Why, yes, sir. We do. But few have a discerning enough palette to ask for it."

"Give me a double-shot please, no ice."

The bartender went off again to fill the order.

"We need to talk," Alexandra hissed.

"But not here," Dmitri countered as the bartender returned and Dmitri put a generous amount on the counter to cover the drinks as well as a tip.

"Why not?"

He inclined his head towards the door. "Because the rest of

the members are coming into this room now for the evening. The DJ has started to play music. And I want to dance with the most beautiful woman I have ever met."

She took a sip from her glass and scowled. "Dance?"

"Yes, you know...we stand close to each other and your body feels what mine is doing, then follows along. It's the closest we can get to fucking in public, while still pretending to be strangers. Of course there's always the danger our bodies are so in tune with each other that it will be obvious to everyone we are lovers..."

Alexandra gulped the rest of the liquid and slammed her glass to the bar. "You're on, big man. Let's see what you've got."

With a smirk, Dmitri downed his double-shot and took her hand to lead her out onto the dance floor to join the first few couples already practicing their ballroom moves. The first few songs were older tunes, the kind that called for more formal dancing. They did a waltz, a quick-step, a fox-trot, and a slow dance that allowed for way more bodily contact than Alexandra was comfortable with, knowing her father and his friends were there watching them.

Shit! He acts like he belongs here more than I do! His manners are impeccable. His small talk entertained everyone all through dinner. And now I find out he's a great ballroom dancer also? He's all of that and yet also still the edgy Russian with dangerous talents and skills that make him a great bouncer in a biker bar. And he fucks like an animal! If I had to pick only one man to have for the rest of my life, I'd want it to be someone like him...

Her train of thought was interrupted as Dmitri took advantage of the steady dimming of the lights that was meant to enhance the mood of those dancing and encourage others to join them. The hand behind her trailed fingers along her spine making her shiver from the contact. He leaned forward to speak directly into her ear, his warm breath raising the hairs along her neck, as a second shiver raced the other one to be the first to warm her clit with memories of pleasure and new anticipation.

"Would anyone think we were being impolite if we were to leave soon? I'm not sure how much longer I can stop myself from bending you over a table and enjoying your screams as I make you come."

A tremor ran through her entire body as every cell lit up with excitement. "Um, I think we could probably use the excuse that I'm going to show you some of the skyline of the Twin Cities at night. Everyone will agree what a good idea that is, while also assuming we're going to head somewhere more private. But no one will call us on it..."

"Not even your father?"

Alexandra arched one eyebrow. "Especially not him. He's the one who introduced us. He'll be hugging himself thinking he finally introduced me to a man I might find interesting. And the fact he's already salivating about the business you might send our way means he'll be anxious to encourage us to continue exploring what we might have in common."

Dmitri's eyes narrowed as the corners of his lips rose. "Then let's tell your father we're leaving and head back to your condo."

As Alexandra had suspected, her father was enthusiastic about the idea of her entertaining Dmitri with a tour of the cities. He shook Dmitri's hand warmly, reminding him that the company now being run by his daughter could handle any business needs the Russian conglomerate might have.

"You should join me for lunch here soon. The chef does a themed lunch here every Thursday. I'm sure he'd be glad to try his hand at Russian delicacies in your honor. You must miss the food you grew up with, being so far from home."

Dmitri smiled. "You have my card. If you email me with the date, I'll try to arrange my schedule to allow for another fine meal at your club."

"Excellent. Good-night, then. Have fun." Thomas turned to his wife to pat her arm dramatically. "Oh, to be young again..."

Alexandra, who was less than ten years younger than her stepmother, smiled inwardly at the fleeting look of jealousy that raced across the other woman's face as Dmitri held her coat for her to slip her arms into and his hands lingered for a moment on her shoulders.

"Good night, Abby. See you soon, Dad."

A few minutes later they stepped outside and Alexandra took a deep breath. "The air is still cold, but it feels good to be out of there, finally." The valet approached them as she asked Dmitri, "Did you drive here?"

Dmitri shook his head, "No, I took a taxi. I figured he'd know how to get here better than me. Plus I didn't plan on going home alone."

Alexandra's lips twitched in amusement. "Cocky, aren't you?"

He bent over to whisper into her ear. "You'd know."

The valet took the ticket she handed him wordlessly and went off to retrieve her vehicle.

"Stop it!" she hissed. "Wait until we can't be seen anymore."

Dmitri shrugged. "No one's watching us out here. Besides, your dad likes me."

"He likes the business he thinks you'll bring us, you mean," she corrected.

"Same thing."

"Is there really any business?"

"There might be..."

The valet pulled up in front of them and opened the driver's side door. With a pointed glance at her passenger, Alexandra strode over to the open door and ignored the valet who was attempting to help her into her seat. Dmitri got in on the other side and they drove off into the night.

* * * *

The elevator ride up from the parking garage wasn't private, since there was an elderly couple with a small, barking dog already in it when the door slid open. Dmitri's eyes were dark with passion whenever Alexandra glanced at his face, and since she was also anxious to be alone with him, she kept looking at the numbers on the wall, willing the elevator to be quicker than usual. It wasn't, but eventually the door slid open on her floor and the tiny dog yapped at them as they walked out. They both walked quickly to her door and Alexandra unlocked it with Dmitri pushing it open from next to her.

Immediately after she locked the door, Alexandra turned to Dmitri and grabbed at the huge bulge tenting out the pleats in the front of his trousers.

"Fuck me now!" She hissed at him.

A small smile played on the corners of his mouth as he shook his head slowly.

"No. That's not how I want to play this out tonight."

"What?" Outrage made her voice higher than its usual low timbre.

"Tonight I was a gentleman in a very exclusive club. I was introduced to the most beautiful woman I've ever met, who allowed me to press myself against her as we danced. She lit a fire inside of my soul that demands satisfaction..."

"Yes." Alexandra rubbed herself against the immovable wall of man in front of her. "Satisfaction...I like the sound of that..."

He put both of his hands over hers where she was busily undoing the knot of his tie.

"Patience, *Sashka*. Tonight I'm not up for simple fucking. I want to make love with the fiery redhead who has captivated my very soul. I want to demonstrate to her how much she has moved this cold, dark, dour Russian man to want to bask in her sunlight. I want her to feel cherished, to let her know how precious she is to me. And making that kind of love takes time."

Alexandra sighed dramatically. "Is this going to take so long I should get myself a drink so I have something to do while I'm waiting for you to finally plow your way into my—"

The corners of his lips rose as he shook his head, covering her lips with a finger to silence her.

"Tonight I plan to worship at the altar of your beauty. I hid a bottle of French Champagne in your fridge yesterday. I'll get it, along with two glasses. Then I'll follow you into the bedroom and seduce you as a gentleman does a lady."

Alexandra rolled her eyes. "Fine. As long as I eventually get laid..."

She turned and headed toward the bedroom with him following right behind her until he turned into the kitchen to grab the supplies.

When he strode into the bedroom a few minutes later carrying the bottle and two crystal flutes, he was amused to see Alexandra had posed herself on the bed, with one leg bent, the other straight out, providing him with an uninterrupted view of her lack of panties. She smiled at him as he put the glasses onto the table next to the bed and began to loosen the cork from the bottle.

"Are you sure you want to take your time, mister?" She purred. "I'm already dripping hot for you...why not take the edge off quickly, then we can take things slower after that?"

He poured the bubbling liquid into the two glasses and handed one to her as he shook his head.

"No, my dear. This is too perfect of an opportunity to resist. We both wear many faces, as I've said before. Tonight is for you to be a lady being seduced by a gentleman. Especially one you didn't expect to find at the club where you are usually bored with the selection of men."

Dmitri sat on the bed next to her and lit the candle next to the bottle before he turned off the lamp. The room was softly illuminated only by a tiny flame. He pulled off his tie and loosened the top buttons of his shirt, then held out his glass and indicated she should clink her glass with his.

"A toast...to the most beautiful woman I have ever had the honor to dance with."

Alexandra took a sip and grinned. "Wow! I've had cheap bubbly and expensive Champagne. This tastes expensive."

He nodded. "It is. Nothing is too much to show you what I think of you."

He spent some time appreciating the view as Alexandra arched her back and stretched sinuously, posing for him, each time inching closer to him.

Dmitri inclined his head towards her feet. "Your feet must be aching in those strappy stiletto heels. I wondered why you were almost taller than me while we were dancing. What are they? Three...four inches?"

"Three and a half. And yes, my feet are killing me!"

"Then why wear them?"

She had moved slowly up to the headboard where Dmitri was leaning back against it, admiring the view. She stretched out one leg and the dress draped back along her thighs, showing him the garters he already knew would be there, along with a glimpse of the expanse of the very white skin of her upper thighs. Dmitri sucked in a breath as he wrestled control away from his rigid cock.

Trying to force his hand, Alexandra casually let one hand move up his thigh until he suddenly pushed himself up to stand, then moved to the end of the bed to sit closer to her feet.

As her face set into a pout, she answered him. "Why? So it will make my legs look sexy...duh! Why do I wear garters when they sometimes dig into my thighs? Same reason."

"And you are so right, *Sashka*," Dmitri murmured softly as he removed one of her shoes, tossed it to the floor, then began to rub her foot. His fingers massaged her arches then moved up to the front pad of her foot, and onto her toes, making her giggle. He moved back to the arch and concentrated on upwards movements that made her moan with pleasure.

"I am?" she asked in a dreamy voice. "That feels so good! The only way I ever get foot rubs is when I pay for a pedicure. And that's over too quickly. You're taking your time and rubbing where it hurts…aah. Don't stop."

He continued to pamper her foot, slowly beginning to include her ankle and calf in the deep-muscle massage.

"Yes," he continued in a low tone. "Your legs were the first things that made me realize I wouldn't be able to hurt you to get you to behave. They convinced me I would have to use more…ah…gently persuasive methods with you. And that would have to involve getting you naked as soon as possible, so I could plunge my cock into you repeatedly until I'd had my fill. Which hasn't happened yet, by the way. It might never happen…not when you show off your legs with garters that end in the creamy white thighs of a natural redhead. I can't resist you…"

Dmitri bent his head to gently kiss her knee as he undid the garters on that leg and rolled the stocking down to toss it aside to join her already discarded shoe. He traced a path with his tongue from her knee up the front of her thigh, then moved to the inside of her thigh and continued to kiss his way up. He inhaled deeply once he was near the furry juncture between her legs and smiled at her as she looked down, regarding him from between half-closed eyelids.

"You are beautiful to look at. Your smell is irresistible. And your taste?" He shuddered, making it obvious he was having difficulty keeping himself under control.

"Then don't wait," Alexandra began, holding out her arms in an invitation.

Dmitri shook his head. "No," he said firmly. "You have another foot that needs tender loving care."

He moved back down to the foot of the bed again and removed her other shoe to repeat the massaging that had given her such exquisite relief on the other foot.

Alexandra sighed with pleasure.

"Yes," Dmitri continued, "I've always had a thing for redheads. And for women with gorgeous legs. Combine those two and I'm in deep trouble."

Alexandra opened her eyes to watch him intently as he moved her up other leg.

"So it was my legs you noticed first? Not my enormous tits?

How? My *girls* are the first part of me to enter a room. I was self-conscious about them for years until I realized just how easily I could get a man to do anything I wanted him to if he thought I would let him grope them..."

Dmitri was already undoing the garters and kissing her second knee as he pulled the second stocking down.

"Not me. I'm a leg man. But I *do* like tits. I'm a man. The nipples are the best part, and yours are almost more than a mouthful. They're also responsive as hell."

He bent his head lower and inhaled again, this time pushing her dress up to her belly so he could trace with both hands a path along her hips while his thumbs massaged her inner thighs. He gently nipped at the tender skin at the crease of her upper thigh and her hips pushed forward as she jumped in surprise.

He looked up at her and smiled, passion darkening his eyes so much they appeared to be a solid black, making him appear dangerous and inhuman.

He slowly licked his way up to her outer lips and sucked both of them into his mouth, his tongue leaving a moist trail to join with the fluids her excitement produced for him. With a quick flick of his tongue, he tapped at her clit and her quick intake of breath was let out with a moan. He got down to serious business with licking and sucking that had her clutching the bedspread with both hands and having many quick-yet-noisy orgasms that let him know how much she appreciated his efforts. As her hips rose up from the bed, he slid both hands under her butt cheeks to hold her up to allow him better access to the inner lips that quivered with the force of her spasms.

After what seemed like hours to her, he gently tapped her thighs.

"Time for you to turn over so I can give you a back massage."

With great difficulty she opened her eyes to stare at him, blinking as she had trouble focusing.

"What? You're leaving me hanging like this?"

His lips twitched as he rose from the bed. "No. I need to use the bathroom. When I get back I want to continue to pamper you. I'll be back in a minute. Drink some more Champagne."

Fuck that man! He's driving me crazy! Alexandra forced her body to respond to commands as she sat up and unhooked her bra, tossing it onto the floor to join her discarded shoes and stockings. She looked down approvingly to see that the soft fabric covering her breasts accentuated her nipples, the peaks hardened even more by the feel of the silk as it moved against them. She reached over to pick up the bottle and poured more Champagne into both of the glasses. She took a few sips from her glass then lay back, one hand idly moving down to stroke herself as she waited. She was just shuddering through an orgasm when he came back into the room and grinned at what he saw.

"That's my girl. Never enough orgasms for you? Don't worry, we're far from done here."

"You took off your shirt," she said breathily, enjoying the sight of his muscular arms and broad shoulders, the wide chest covered in curly black hair that trailed down to his abs as if leading her to look even further down to where the huge bulge tented out his pleated slacks.

He sat on the side of the bed next to the bottle and took a long drink from his glass before putting it back down again. He leaned over and began to kiss her shoulder, his one hand resting on her thigh, the other one pulling off the shoulder strap on that side, as he pulled the one closest to him off with his teeth. Both straps were off but the silky dress stayed mostly in place, held up by her breasts that were now exposed almost to the nipples.

"They are magnificent breasts," he breathed into her ear, making the tiny hairs stand up as she shivered with pleasure. One large hand moved to cup a breast in the palm, his fingers rubbing and tweaking the nipple that was already pursed with excitement. He leaned forward and his mouth covered the nipple closer to him as he licked then suckled her through the thin fabric. She continued to twitch with excitement, pressing her upper thighs closer together, enjoying the after-shocks of her recent orgasms.

He chuckled softly as he noticed her movements. He pinched one nipple and bit the other one, making her yelp.

"Now you need to roll over for your massage."

"Do I have to?" She began with a whine, but obediently began to turn herself over. Once she was on her stomach Dmitri got up to move around to stand next to the side of the bed she lay on. He reached under her stomach to pull her up onto her hands and knees. When she turned and looked at him with a challenge in her eyes he shook his head.

"Not yet. I need to get your dress off before I can do a proper back massage."

The tiny noise of disappointment she made was swallowed abruptly when after unzipping her dress and pulling it down, his fingers began to push into her dripping hole, making her gnash her teeth with frustration.

"More! I need more!"

"And that's what you'll get...when I'm ready. Now lie back face down. I'm going to make your muscles release all of that nasty tension you've been working under for so long."

As she spoke she wondered what was taking him so long. "Then we can fuck like animals?"

"No, then we're going to be wilder than animals...we'll fuck like the wild things we both are."

She felt the bed move as he moved up onto it next to her, then she heard a click as if a bottle was being opened. He began to rub her shoulders and upper back with both hands and she inhaled deeply.

"What is that? It smells delicious..."

"Almond massage lotion. I think it smells relaxing yet arousing...if that kind of oxymoron is possible."

Alexandra sighed with contentment as he continued to work at her tense shoulder muscles, massaging out knots that had been there for so long she'd forgotten they weren't a permanent part of her anatomy.

"If I didn't know better I'd have no idea you were from another country. You speak English better than lots of guys I know."

"How so?"

"Most would have no idea what an oxymoron even *is*, let alone be able to make a comparison like that."

"I went to good schools and I read a lot. I always wanted to come to the US to see for myself if the *Great Satan* was either great or the devil's work."

"And is it?"

He continued rubbing her back, his hands moving onto her lower back, his fingers beginning to massage her glutes. It seemed to be only accidental that his movements were spreading her cheeks to allow massage oil to penetrate both of her openings.

"It's not the Satanic Empire I was taught to believe it was, that's for sure. I'm not sure it's great, but I do know that having lived here for a while, I have no plans to go anywhere else. There's still too much to experience."

The bed moved as Dmitri repositioned himself and Alexandra gasped as she felt his entire body lying on top of her, still moving around.

From very close to her ear Dmitri asked, "How do you like the full body rub?"

"You mean you rub my body with yours?"

"*Da*. And you continue to respond like that…"

Alexandra started to squirm, feeling him beginning to press his hips forward to rub himself against her slippery entrance. She tried to anticipate his movements, to trap him into pushing forward at the right time. She was rewarded by the feeling of being forced open as the wide head pushed into her and she squeezed hard, trying to hold him inside of her.

"Is this what you want, *Sashka*?" Dmitri asked before he pushed forward in a deliberately slow manner: the wide head followed by the rock hard shaft made her tremble with pleasure each time he was inside of her. He was stopped by her cervix, then he pulled back only to re-enter her more forcibly each time.

"Yes…oh, yes! More! More!"

She was already trembling through a multiple orgasm when he drew himself back up to position himself on his knees between her thighs. He pulled her hips up and he pistoned himself in and out of her. She hardly noticed one hand had let go until she felt something begin to push at her darker opening. He continued to slam himself into her as he continued his twin assault on her. She felt his fingers still digging into her hip and realized it was his thumb wriggling its way into her anus. She began to moan louder as she felt herself climbing a mountain of pleasure, with something big definitely on the other side.

With a scream she fell off the other side into an abyss of orgasmic sensations! Every cell in her body exploded as she squeezed her eyes shut to watch the fireworks in her brain. She shuddered and trembled, every muscle in her body twitching in unison as she rode her orgasms to higher and higher explosions.

Dmitri had felt her getting close. *About damn time! I can't keep this up much longer! So tight…so wet…so hot…I can feel my thumb with my cock! Oh…my …God! Here I go…*

His fingers dug into her as he pulled her close, jamming himself as deeply into her welcoming heat as he could, feeling her trembling walls steal his last vestige of control as he gave himself over to the force of his own bliss. The hot blast burned as it shot out of him, every muscle in his body tensed before the cataclysmic release that made him howl with the intensity of his pleasure.

They were locked like that for what seemed like an eternity. Each one uttered harsh sounds as they came, which would make the other tremble again, which would urge the other to shiver. They had aftershocks together for so long that when finally Dmitri collapsed on her back, he had no strength to hold his weight off of her to allow her to breathe. For her part, Alexandra was floating out of consciousness, in a cloud of orgasmic bliss that didn't require her to do anything so plebeian as breathe. She had passed out.

It was a very long time later that Dmitri rolled off to the one side and gently stroked Alexandra's cheek with one finger. He pushed back the hair that covered her face and was momentarily frightened by the depth of emotion he felt as he stared at her, watching her breathing deeply, her lips red from her biting them in the throes of passion.

I've fallen in love with you, Sashka, he acknowledged ruefully. *Now I have to be sure you fall in love with me also. Not just temporarily, but for good. You have to belong to me alone. There is no other way.*

Alexandra sighed as she opened one eye. She noticed he was staring at her and she smiled.

"Yes, I'm still alive," she said in a voice husky from screaming. "Barely. I think I passed out for a while."

He nodded. "Yes, you did. I might have also."

She pushed herself around to lie on her side and he pulled her closely into his arms. She blew at the chest hair tickling her nose then bit the nipple closest to her.

"That was some world-class fucking, big guy! You are amazing!"

He smiled. "Not getting bored with me yet, huh?"

She shook her head slowly, then regarded him closely. "No. And that in itself is amazing."

He reached over to tweak her nipple. "Ready for round two?"

She laughed then had a coughing fit. She reached for her

glass and he grabbed the bottle. She took a long sip to finish what was in her glass and he refilled it, then poured the last of the bottle for himself. He picked up his glass and clinked it against hers again.

"To us. May we never get bored with each other."

She stared at him searchingly, then nodded before she took another long drink.

"How about we have the next few rounds tomorrow? Every cell in my body is tired right now. You never told me before you have magic hands. I've never felt so exhausted in my life. I could sleep for a hundred years."

He smiled. "I have to keep the magic in my hands a secret. Otherwise women all over the world would be clamoring for a massage. I'd never get any rest."

Alexandra let out an uncharacteristic giggle. "Their loss. My gain."

Dmitri took her empty glass from her hand and leaned over to put both flutes on the bed-stand. He blew out the candle and turned to lie on his back. Alexandra moved closer to him and he reached out his arm to pull her into an embrace. They lay silently for a while, each listening to the sound of the other breathing.

"Dmitri? You asleep?"

"Almost. Why?"

"Thanks."

He smiled into the darkness. "For what?"

"Just...thanks."

When he didn't reply, she said, "I don't always know what I need. Or what I want. But you seem to..."

"Um-hmm," he agreed.

She listened to his breathing take on the regular rhythm of sleep as he drifted off.

I never thought I could enjoy just one man so much...

Her breathing soon regulated itself into a sleep pattern as the first rays of the rising sun began to slip through the cracks of her blinds.

Chapter Nine

As they enjoyed their after-dinner drunken coffees the next night, Dmitri took a deep breath before he spoke.

"So, I'm going out of town for a few days…" he began.

Alexandra's eyes widened in surprise. "A few days? How long is a few days?"

He shrugged. "I dunno. Maybe a week. Maybe longer. Depends…"

"On what?" Her tone sharpened.

"On how long I need to take care of business."

"What kind of business?"

He cocked his head to meet her gaze. "It's not your concern. I'll let you know when I'm on my way back."

"So, are you acting as a hit man for your cousin? Heading out of town to kill someone, then you'll appear back here as if nothing special happened?"

His eyes narrowed. "Is that really what you think of me?"

Alexandra shrugged. "I don't know what to think of you. If you'll remember, I met you when you were sent to…*teach me a lesson*, I think was the way you put it. You told me you had put a major hurt on the men you were sent after. Now you tell me you're going out of town on *business*. But the only job you have here is being a bouncer on weeknights at a biker bar. That's not the kind of business you'd need to go out of town for."

"I did tell your father I represented a conglomerate of Russian companies."

"I thought that was just bullshit to impress my dad."

"And I told you it was partly true. Maybe I have to do a few things to be sure it's all true. Otherwise your father is going to wonder why I'm hanging around his daughter so much."

Alexandra snorted. "Honey, men have been hanging around his daughter since middle school, when my tits started growing and didn't stop until I was almost too big for a double D!"

He nodded. "Of course. But this trip will combine a few things I need to get done. I've been putting it off because I've been enjoying spending so much time with you. But I need to look at the bigger picture and that means I've got some things to take care of."

"So, you're not gonna just go whack some guy your cousin Ivan, the ex KGB-agent, told you to?"

In defense, he attacked. "Why the sudden interest in my affairs? I don't ask what you're doing at your office all day. Or on the nights I'm not here."

"Working. And working out then resting so I'll be up for multiple rounds of energetic fucking when I see you the next time. So there!" She stuck out her tongue at him.

Dmitri smiled. "If you really want me to account for my days and nights, I'll call you and fill you in."

He watched as a myriad of emotions played themselves out on her face.

She's nosy…she's jealous…and she appears to be anxious. She doesn't want me to go. Maybe she'll be willing to give up any pretense of needing other men. Maybe she'll realize she doesn't need any other men when she has me.

Alexandra's lips twitched upwards before she spoke. "Well, at least it's supposed to be warm enough to ride this weekend. That means we'll be headed out to my place up by Mille Lacs. I'll probably get the gang to ride up there with me on Saturday and we can get the place aired out and open for the season."

Dmitri's face set in stone as he remembered what he'd been told about the pleasure room in the barn. He firmly clamped down on his rising jealousy.

She'll head out there with the gang? There'll be group sex and orgies going on? Other dicks will be fucking my woman?

He realized she had stopped talking and was staring at him now, trying to read his face.

He doesn't look happy about me heading out to the farm with the gang. I wonder if someone's been talking to him, telling him what we do out there. Too bad. He's gonna be gone, probably fucking other women. What does he expect me to do? Sit around playing with myself waiting for him? I'm not a commitment kind of gal…

"Alexandra…" he began in a stern voice.

"What? I'm not *Sashka* to you anymore? You Russians are so funny with your multiple names…"

"That's how you know I'm being serious. I've heard about the kinds of things you do with your gang when you go out to your farm. I'm not sure I want you going there without me…"

"Well, you're going to be out of town, so tough shit. I won't know how many other women you'll be fucking while you're gone, so try not to think about what I'll be doing."

"My business is going to keep me too busy to look for women to fuck. Besides, the only woman I'm interested in is you."

"Well I'm not a one-man kind of woman. I don't do monogamy. Marriage is a cheap-ass legal maneuver thought up by a man to keep the little woman horny at home while he goes out and cocks a leg over whatever pussy catches his eye. I swore years ago no man is going to make a fool out of me like my dad did to my mom. She still can't figure out what she did wrong. I've tried to explain to her he's just a pig. Most men are. The only way to stay safe is to not let any man get the upper hand. Fuck any you want to, and make sure they know that's what you're doing. They can either accept me the way I am, or get the fuck out of my way."

She glared at him defiantly, with her arms crossed over her chest.

"What if you change your mind?"

"I won't."

"Is there any way you'd reconsider?"

"No."

"Nothing I can do to make you feel differently?"

Alexandra shook her head. "Nope. And don't even bother asking me to come with you out of town. Now I'd see through that as a way to keep me fucking only you."

"I wasn't planning on asking you to accompany me. The things I've got to do require me to travel light…alone. But in case you haven't noticed, I've been the only one in your bed lately."

She smiled over her coffee cup at him. "None of my gang has ever been in my bed here. No one even knows where my condo is. That's part of how I keep my different personas separate. *You* are the only one who knows where I live…you're the only one who's slept here with me, and you're the only one I've let fuck me without a condom. That's already way more concessions than you deserve, considering I don't really know much about you."

He bowed his head slightly. "I'm honored. What more do you want to know about me?"

"Oh, I don't know. How about, where did you grow up?"

"On a farm in a small town near Minsk. My father was a farmer."

"I thought your family business was being KGB agents."

"That's from my mom's side of the family."

Alexandra laughed. "Your mom? No wonder you can handle a strong woman!"

Dmitri's lips twitched as he nodded. "Yup. Dad taught me how to farm, but Mom taught me how to fight and how to shoot while I was still a young boy."

"And how to pick locks?"

"Nah...I picked that up along the way from other kids who were older than me and didn't mind teaching me stuff like that if I shared what I knew about fighting."

"So, your cousin up in Grand Marais...he's from your mom's side?"

"*Da*. He's her brother's oldest son. When I was old enough for college he invited me to move into his apartment with him in Moscow. That's where my education really began...both academically in my classes, and through what I learned from him. He told me I was the most promising of his cousins and he had high hopes for me. The Iron Curtain had been torn down when I was a kid, but the country was still in upheaval from the fall-out. The collapse of the Communist government meant no one was really in charge, and those who worked for the KGB were skilled enough to be sure they were always in on whatever action was happening. I met a lot of the old ones, those who had stories even more hair-raising than Ivan's. But it was from him I learned the most about how to work the system...any system, to come out ahead."

"And he was the one who sponsored you into the US?"

His lips twitched again. "Uh...yeah...in a way."

Her eyes narrowed. "You're not here legally, are you?"

"What is that thing you people say? *I refuse to answer on the grounds it may incriminate me.*"

"So that's why as smart and educated as you are, you're working as a bouncer in a biker bar?"

"Actually no. *You* are the reason I'm working as a bouncer in a biker bar. You're the only reason I'm still in this city. If I wasn't enjoying you, I'd be long gone."

"To where?"

Dmitri shrugged. "It's a big country. Anywhere I want to go."

They drank their coffees in silence for a few minutes, both still too busy digesting dinner to want to move off the couch.

Alexandra sighed. "I've never lied to you. I told you from the start I'm not interesting in being part of a monogamous couple."

"Yes, you did. But I'm still holding out hope that you just hadn't met the right man yet. Until now."

They stared into each other's eyes for a while, both trying to read the other's thoughts, neither having any success.

Finally Alexandra broke the silence. "Are you coming back?"

"That's my plan."

"So you're not giving up on me?"

"Not yet. When I do, you'll know. I'll be gone."

He leaned forward to run his fingers through her hair, his hand traveling to the back of her head as he leaned further forward and covered her lips with his for a long, passionate kiss.

He drew back slightly and looked into her eyes, their noses almost touching.

"Will you miss me?"

She licked her lips, the slight movement of her tongue darting out of her mouth making his cock twitch, even though they had spent the better part of the last twenty-four hours having sex in every position they could imagine.

"Um…I won't know until you're gone."

"Fair enough."

Dmitri stood up and picked up the coffee pot and his cup.

"Let's soak in the Jacuzzi for a while, then make wild passion one more time before we sleep. I know you have to be up early tomorrow, and I'll be leaving when you do because I have an early flight."

Alexandra was able to temporarily ignore the thoughts whirling around in her head as she followed him down the hall. They were soon involved in sexual acrobatics so intense she had no time to think about anything else.

But much later that night as they lay close together in the darkness, she stared at the ceiling while she listened to him drifting off to sleep.

He's going to be gone. He might not come back. If he does and I've been with other men will he leave for good? Why should I care? He's just another man with a huge dick. Plenty more of them around. Men are replaceable. There's always one with a bigger dick right around the corner, waiting for me...right? And in the meantime I've got my gang. None of them are as hung as he is, but I've always had plenty of orgasms with them. Nothing like having one man slamming into your hole while you suck another guy off...right? I'll be fine. I won't miss him that much. Right?

She tossed and turned for a while before finally falling asleep. She woke up feeling exhausted and not at all looking forward to the new week.

Chapter Ten

On Wednesday night when the phone rang as she was running on the treadmill, Alexandra thought about just letting it ring. But she had a feeling it might be Dmitri calling, so she jumped off the machine and grabbed it off of her table before the sixth ring took it to voicemail. A quick glance at it told her she was right.

"Hello?" She was panting from exertion and hoarse, so she grabbed her water bottle and gulped a few times.

"Hello, Alexandra. I hope your out-of-breath condition only indicates you were working out, not entertaining in my absence."

"Ha ha, Mister Smart-ass. If I was entertaining I wouldn't have answered the phone."

"I see. Well I'm glad you did. It's Wednesday and I've been lying on my hotel room bed thinking about you and how we usually pass our time on Wednesday nights."

"Why do you think I'm working out so hard, asshole? You won't be coming over later to ease my stress, so I've gotta take care of things myself."

"And I have no doubt you will, later. As will I."

"Too bad you didn't call later. We could have phone sex and orgasm together, even if it's long-distance."

"Do you want me to hang up and call back later?"

"No. It's good to hear your voice."

"Can I take that to mean you miss me?"

"Yeah...well, I mean I miss your huge cock, anyway."

"It *is* attached to me, so I'll take that as a compliment."

"You do that."

"So one of the reasons I called is to get directions to that place of yours, just in case I get back into the area early enough to be able to meet you out there on Saturday."

"I thought you were going to be gone longer."

"Things are going well and I might be done sooner than I anticipated."

"Do you have a piece of paper and something to write with?"

"Yes."

"Okay, then. You need to take 694 west until it turns into 94, then head north on 101 until it turns into 169. Take that north until you hit 27 and head east. You'll be right under Mille Lacs Lake then. When you hit the town of Bayview, head south on the only road you can, then right before it ends turn left and the driveway for my place will be where the road ends. The mailbox says Blackstone. You'll be able to see the house from there, and there will be bikes parked all over the place."

"Got it. Will you be happy to see me, if I can manage to get there Saturday night?"

"Yeah. I'll be keeping it juicy just for you."

"Woman, you torture me."

"I know, right? See you soon?"

"*Da.*"

"Okay, then, big guy. I've gotta finish my work-out before I run out of energy. I'm trying to get myself in riding shape, so I'm pushing harder than usual. You just keep on thinking about me, and yell out my name when you come. I'll be listening for it."

Dmitri chuckled. "Fine. Good night, you gorgeous vixen."

She smiled. "Good-night to you, Boris Badenov."

* * * *

Dmitri caught a late night flight out of O'Hare on Friday. As he stared out at the dark night, he thought over what he had accomplished during his time in Chicago.

That woman Ivan put me in touch with seems really good. What a coincidence I'd met her before. Since she remembered me from our long-ago encounter, when I did her a favor, she's going to do her best to assure I'll be a legal alien on a visitor's visa by next week. Nice to know those who used to be enemies can put aside old grievances and help out a fellow agent. Ivan got himself legal using her and he's been here so long he's a citizen now. If I'm going to stay for the long-term, I need to be sure I won't have to keep moving. Plus once I'm legal, I can register as the representative for the Russian companies Ivan put me in touch with who are trying to break into the US market. That will make old man

Blackstone happy enough to welcome me into the family... presuming I can get his wildcat of a daughter to agree.

His mind wandered off for a while as he amused himself with images of what he planned to do to celebrate his wedding night with the redhead he craved, once he got her to agree to give up other men for a steady diet of energetic fucking, Russian-style. His cock responded as it did whenever he even thought of her and aware of the fact that most of the other passengers around him were asleep, he spent some time adjusting himself to avoid injury from the zipper on his suddenly way-too-tight jeans.

Tomorrow I'll rent a bike and follow her directions out to the family farm. I just hope I don't find her fucking any of the other guys. I'll have to control myself so I don't hurt anyone... too much. I'm running out of ideas on how to convince her that the only man she needs is me. If she starts having fun with the others in her gang again, she may forget just how good it is between us. I'm not ready to give up on her...yet. But there's only so much I can take...

He went back to moodily staring out the window at the passing of the dark sky.

* * * *

Dmitri didn't have any trouble getting a hold of a bike. He called the guy his boss told him to call, and the man was only too happy to dispense with filling out any paperwork since he didn't balk at the amount of cash he was asked to fork over. The only real problem was Dmitri had never ridden a Harley before. He was able to get it off the lot and out in the street, but it handled differently from any other motorcycle he'd ever been on before. He found an empty parking lot and spent some time learning how it rode, how it took turns, how it felt when it changed gears, etc.

Since he hadn't slept on the plane, he'd gotten a late start in the morning. After he felt comfortable with the Harley, he set off in the early afternoon, heading up for the family place Alexandra used for her gang's party-house. It was a couple of hours later that Dmitri pulled up to the house with her name on the mailbox. As she had predicted there were bikes parked all around the house, so he rode up and parked his as well.

He strode up to the house and yelled into it when he tried the door handle and found it open.

"Hello! Anyone home?"

He heard a female voice yelling from the back of the house.

"Back here! I'm in the kitchen. Come on back."

He followed the voice and walked into a cozy farm kitchen that immediately reminded him of home. There was the aroma of baked goods and other foods cooking and he smiled at the sight of a dark-haired female bending over to get something out of the oven. She turned around to put the brownies on a cooking rack and smiled back at him.

"Hey, Dmitri. Alex said you might be coming out here today. In fact she seemed kind of disappointed you weren't already here. She was afraid you might have gotten lost somewhere."

"I'm sorry, but I don't remember your name..." he began.

"I'm Emma. I'm the one who used to work for Alex but left to open my own bakery. She helped bankroll me and in return she owns part of my business. I'm not making much of a profit yet, but business is steady, so it's all good."

Dmitri nodded. "I remember. She told me you used to be married to an abuser and she helped you out of a bad situation."

The woman nodded then sat on one of the chairs at the long table and took a long swallow from the plastic cup of beer near her. She waved at the other chairs.

"Sit. Take a load off. I can't yak for long since I'm still working on dinner, but I can take a breather."

"Where is everyone?"

She smiled. "What you mean is where's Alex, right? They're all out in the barn, partying. We got up here hours ago. We opened all the windows to air out the house, turned on the water, the electricity and the gas, and put sheets on the beds. The keg is tapped, the case of Reverend Jack is open and she started on her own personal bottle hours ago. "

Dmitri heard himself growling as he tried to keep his face neutral.

"You're not happy about her fucking the other guys," Emma made it a statement of fact.

"No," was the only word he could choke out as he struggled with the desire to rush out and see for himself what was going on.

Emma reached over and patted his arm. "She's never been in love, dude. She has no idea what it's like to want one person so much you can't imagine being with anyone else. Her old man's betrayal of her mom cut her deeply since she was an impressionable teenager then. She's never felt the same about him since. Because of him she doesn't trust men. She thinks you're all cheating pigs. To keep herself from getting hurt, she never lets any of you close enough to matter. Making you all share her is her way of keeping control over you and keeping herself pain free."

He looked away from her, taking deep breaths, trying to control his anger before he went out to the barn.

"You're not listening to me, are you?"

He turned to stare at her. "You're not saying anything I don't already know. But I don't share. Either I get all of her, or I'm out of here."

She shook her head, whistling softly.

"You *are* the different one, aren't you? She's missed you this week. She was talking about you almost constantly when we got here, wondering when you'd get here, worrying you'd get lost. Give her time. You just might be the one man who can get through to her, but she won't make it easy."

He pushed himself up from the chair. "Which way is the barn?"

She waved to indicate the direction.

"Go out the back door and look to your right. You can't miss it." She studied his face. "You sure you don't want a drink before you go? I don't want you hurting anyone when you get out there..."

He glared at her. "I don't plan to."

"Okay. Just remember she's missed you, but she'll be fighting anything she feels because it's not a normal way to be for her."

Dmitri nodded at her and strode quickly to the door. Emma watched as his pace quicken the closer he got to the barn.

"I sure hope you can control yourself when you get there," she said aloud as he opened the door and went into the barn. "She's gonna fight against your wanting her to yourself. If you hold on long enough, you might win. Good luck with that."

She turned off the timer and got back to working on dinner for the crowd, sure to be hungry after satisfying every other appetite.

* * * *

Dmitri stopped when he got to the side door of the barn and took a few moments searching for the quiet place in his mind, to enter as calmly as possible. He took a deep breath and pushed the door open to find scenes that made him suddenly feel over-dressed. He also felt like his pants were two sizes too small as the zipper pressed into his turgid flesh. He'd been in whorehouses in many countries, so he wasn't shocked as much as surprised at the variety of goings-ons. The room seemed dark after the late afternoon sunlight, so he looked around for a few minutes while his eyes adjusted.

Angela, the Hispanic woman he'd danced with was in his view first, her wrists in manacles attached to the wall. She was completely nude and her eyes were tightly shut as a man who appeared Hispanic from the color of his skin and hair, plowed into her repeatedly. Both his hands gripped her hips and he held her away from the wall so he was supporting her weight with his hips.

That must be José, the guy she rides with.

Katie, the small blonde woman was on her hands and knees on a hay bale, with a tall dark-haired man fucking her ass with gusto. She grunted each time he pushed fully into her, while she was lustily sucking the cock of the shorter man who stood before her, tugging on the nipples of her pendulous breasts that jiggled like Jell-O each time she was pushed forward.

That accounts for Katie and two more of the men...I think their names are Jim and Chuck. Still no Alexandra? Where is she?

He walked a few steps and saw even more scenes being enacted. There was music blasting into the barn, but no one appeared to be paying any attention to the steady rock beat or the singer rasping out what he planned to do to the women of the world.

A tall blond man was getting his cock sucked by a brunette woman who was lying on her back on another hay bale. There was a man standing in-between her legs, eagerly licking and sucking on her pussy while using a vibrator to make her moan around the cock in her mouth.

That blond guy's Steve and Brad's making Valerie come... hope she doesn't bit down hard while she's twitching or she'll hurt someone.

The man named Rich who had spoken to Dmitri in the bar

was forcefully using a riding crop to raise welts on the ass of the only other woman in the gang, who had both of her wrists tied together and attached to a metal ring on the wall, while she was bent over yet another hay bale. His turgid cock was red and angry-looking, with pre-cum dripping from it. As Dmitri watched he suddenly rammed himself into the woman and she stopped whimpering in pain to begin to shriek with pleasure.

Holy-fucking shit! Rich is all but attacking her...her name's Leann, I think. But where is Alexandra?

Suddenly her voice rang out from just ahead of him, where she was sitting on a bale of hay with another at her back for her to lean against. She was wearing a black corset that laced up the front, and ended just below the expanse of her white breasts, which spilled over the top. She held a bottle of booze in one hand and a joint in the other as she smiled at him, seemingly oblivious to the blond man whose head bobbed as he energetically licked and sucked at her pussy.

"Hey Dmitri! You finally got here! Bring that big, wide cock of yours over here and fuck me silly! I've been waiting for you! No one else has fucked me today yet, so you could be my first. C'mon and do me right! Show my gang what you've got!"

He might have been imagining things, but it seemed as if even the music volume was lowered. The sounds from all of the participants seemed to be quieter, as if everyone was waiting for him to act.

Do I kill him? No! I want to stay in this country! Do I fuck her? And become just another one of her man? Hell no! I'm so fucking hard I'd come as soon as I shoved into that dripping, tight hole of hers! I'm so fucked...coming here was a mistake!

Dmitri cleared his throat to speak, trying to wrestle control over his emotions that demanded actions he didn't want to have to answer for.

"Sorry, Alexandra. I don't do crowds and I don't share. I've told you that."

She pouted, her lips looking so plump he wanted to rush over and kiss her, sucking them into his mouth, or pushing his cock in past them.

"But I want you! I want your cock! You're my main man, Dmitri! C'mon and make me scream!"

He shook his head slowly. "No. I don't share. When you're ready to be with just *me* again, call me."

With that he spun around quickly and strode out of the barn, past all of the curious faces of the men who either sneered at him or had surprise written on their faces, and the women who gave him lustful glances.

"If you walk out that door don't bother coming back! If you turn me down now, don't expect to fuck me again!" Alexandra's shriek had a desperate edge to it.

Dmitri kept walking until he was out of the barn, letting the door slam closed behind him. He was aware he was panting as he strode quickly over to the rented bike, started it up, and headed out into the waning daylight. As he got to the road that led to the long driveway, he passed another biker who gave him the closed fist salute used by Harley riders. Grimly he returned the greeting then switched to a higher gear and headed for the highway.

* * * *

Bob parked his bike and pulled the groceries he'd gone out for, out of his saddle-pack. He bounded up the stairs and quickly moved to the kitchen. Emma looked up, smiled as she heard him enter and she opened her arms. He threw the bag onto the table and pulled her into a tight embrace.

"I got what you needed, woman," he began after a long, lingering kiss.

"You got that right, mister. You do have what I need," she answered in a teasing tone. "But did you get the extra eggs and chocolate chips so I can make more cookies?"

He nodded. His hands trailed down her back and stopped when he grabbed both of her butt cheeks, kneading the ample flesh and grinding himself against her.

"Down, boy!" She lightly pushed him back. "I've still got baking to do!"

"Just my luck I fall in love with the cook! Everyone else is fucking like wild animals and I'm in here watching you make food."

Her eyebrows rose. "You could head on out to the barn, you know. Nothing's stopping you."

He shook his head. "Nothing but the fact that I'm so head-over-heels in love with you I'm not even sure I could get hard for anyone else anymore."

She grinned. "I'll bet you could. You never seem to have any trouble with that..."

He grinned back. "That's because when I'm with you, I don't. I'll just go get us more beer and be right back."

Emma nodded at him and squinted at another recipe as she tore open the bag of chocolate chips.

Bob stuck his head back in the doorway to ask. "Hey, did I just see Alex's man Dmitri leaving? When'd he get here?"

Emma stared at him. "He was leaving? He just went out to the barn looking for her! I've got a bad feeling about this..."

Bob nodded. "I'll get back quickly with the beer."

* * * *

Alexandra had never felt so humiliated in her life.

What the fuck? Everyone's here watching and he just walked out on me? I turned down all of the other guys...some of the best fucks I've ever had, so he could be the first one of the day and he walked out on me?

Tom, the barely-bearded biker who was licking her pussy had stopped and was stroking himself into full hardness as he pulled on a condom.

"Who the fuck needs him, my queen? You're so juicy right now I can't wait to feel you gripping me so hard..."

She sat up and crossed her legs together.

"What? No! I've been waiting for his fat choad all this time and he turned me down? Who the fuck does he think he is? I'm so pissed off right now I don't think I could come for anyone!" She took a huge gulp from her bottle and belched loudly.

The tall man with the riding crop pulled out of the woman he'd been fucking and strode over.

"Trade ya, Tom. No offense, dude but I've got a bigger cock than you. If the queen wants a big one, I'm her man."

"You're not listening," Alexandra said as she pushed herself off the hay bale and stood up, swaying slightly from being upright again, and from the bottle in her hand that was already half-empty.

"I said I don't want to fuck anyone right now. I'm too pissed. I've gotta pee and get me another bottle. I think I'm gonna get really shit-faced tonight. That fucker has issues and he's harshing my buzz. I need some time to process..."

She pushed past the two men who watched as she staggered over to the door and opened it. She stopped while she was in the door frame and yelled back over her shoulder, "But don't let that stop any of the rest of you! There's enough holes in there for everyone to get his rocks off. My bitches are as horny as my bikers, right? Orgasms for everyone!"

"Yeah, except you," Rich said in a low growl as he watched her leave. He turned back to find Tom had already inserted himself into the woman he'd been whipping and pleasuring. He quickly made his way to where her face was, pulling off the condom as he walked. Once he was in front of her, he yanked at her hair and rubbed his cock on her face. She looked up and him and smiled, opening her mouth to swallow him. He pushed in so far she gagged, then he pulled out and began fucking her face, taking his irritation out on her throat.

* * * *

The back door slammed open and Alexandra stumbled into the kitchen. "Man, I gotta pee so bad my teeth are floating!" She had her hand on the door handle of the pantry that had been converted into a bathroom, when it was suddenly opened and she started in surprise.

"Bob! Outta my way!" She pushed past him and slammed the door behind her.

Bob walked back in, his eyebrows raised in a silent question to Emma. She shrugged and shook her head. He sat in one of the chairs at the table and watched her making cookie dough.

Alexandra flung open the bathroom door and entered the room dramatically.

"Men! Who the fuck can understand what the hell they're thinking? They all want free pussy, they all want to fuck, then you give them what they want and they're not happy!" She took a long swallow from her bottle and peered into it closely.

"Hey, I'm about done with this bottle. Bob, be a sweetie and grab me another one, okay?"

He got up and went into the next room while Emma sliced the brownies and offered a couple on a napkin to her errant queen.

"Here, Alex. You need to eat something. It's gonna be a while before dinner's ready and you're racing through the Jack like there's no tomorrow. You don't want to pass out before the campfire, do you?"

"I don't care! I don't care about anything anymore," she

pouted, but she broke a piece off of one of the brownies and shoved it into her mouth.

"So where's Dmitri? Didn't he find you in the barn?" She regretted the words the instant they'd left her lips.

Alexandra's eyes were twin flames of anger as she slammed her bottle back down after washing the cake down with another huge gulp.

"Yeah, that fucker found me all right. And when I invited him to pull out his big fat dick and fuck me hard, 'cause I've been missing him so bad, he said *no*! Can you believe that? He fuckin' said *no*! In front of everyone!"

Bob had come back into the room and put another bottle on the table next to the almost empty one.

"Why the fuck did he ride all the way up here, knowing I'd be fucking my gang…then when he gets here and I'm only getting head from Tom, he gets all high and mighty, and stomps out?" She gulped the last of the first bottle as she finished swallowing the last piece of the second brownie, then she pulled the second bottle closer.

"Did he tell you why? What did he say?" Bob shot a glance at Emma who nodded at him from behind Alexandra.

"He said he didn't share. That I should call him when I was ready to be with only him. The fucking nerve! Who the fuck does he think he is? Does he think I'm some sweet, needy, little fucking woman who's dumb enough to fall in love with him?"

Emma cleared her throat. "Well, honey, he does care a lot about you. I could tell that from the look on his face when he got here and he asked where you were. He was trying to control his temper, but you could see in his face he wanted to kill someone when I told him you were in the barn."

Alexandra exploded. "Does he really think I'm that fucking stupid? After what I saw my mom go through? No man is ever gonna have that kind of power over me! I'm the one who calls the shots! I'm in control! No man can resist me when I want them! Right, Bob?"

As if she just realized he was there, she suddenly leaned back in her chair and began to fondle her nipples with both hands, squirming in her chair. "I mean, you'd fuck me any time I asked, right?"

Bob shot a quick look at Emma and cleared his throat.

"Um, about that…" he began hesitantly.

Alexandra looked at him expectantly.

Emma spoke up. "We were planning on telling everyone after dinner, around the campfire."

Alexandra turned to stare at her. "Telling everyone what?"

Bob blurted out. "We're getting married!"

"*What?*"

Emma nodded, coming around to sit on the chair next to Alexandra and pat her knee.

"Why do you think Bob's in here instead of out in the barn?"

Alexandra continued to stare uncomprehendingly at first one then the other.

"I've known for a long time Emma was special. I just didn't know if she felt the same way," Bob spoke quickly, as if relieved he could share his emotions, while at the same time explaining his behavior in a way that Alexandra wouldn't be insulted.

"Over the winter we spent a lot of time together…just the two of us. I asked her to marry me last week. It was Mother's Day and I gave her my mom's engagement ring, telling her I'd never loved another woman so much, since my mom passed away. But Emma is so special that I just know this is the right thing for us."

Emma nodded. "We were hoping we could do the wedding up here. Make it a biker celebration. At least the reception. I'm okay with a courthouse ceremony. I had the whole church thing the last time and after such a huge build-up, it ended up being a disaster. I'd rather the ceremony was quiet and small this time, and hopefully the marriage will last longer."

Bob smiled at her. "It will. I know you're the only woman I want for the rest of my life."

Alexandra was still staring open-mouthed at them.

Emma giggled. "Stop staring at us, Alex! It can't be that much of a surprise! Other people get married all of the time! Aren't you happy for us?"

Alexandra pulled the cap off the second bottle and took a long drink from it before she answered.

"Yeah, I guess. It's just that I figured that after Craig and Mike took off last summer, that we wouldn't lose any more riders for a while."

"You're not losing either of us, Alex," Emma said as she patted her knee again. "We're still going to ride with the gang. The only difference is that like now, when you're in the barn fucking up a storm, we'll be in here. I'll be cooking and baking..."

"And I'll be entertaining her with stupid jokes and bad puns," Bob said. "I'll also be admiring the most beautiful woman in the world, who belongs to me."

Alexandra's eyes widened as she watched him lean over and give a loving kiss to Emma. Suddenly the timer went off and Emma jumped up to pull a tray of cookies out of the oven and shove another one in.

Alexandra shook her head. "You know, I've watched all of my crew fucking like rabbits. I've fucked all of the men and watched while they made other women scream with pleasure. But I don't think I've ever felt as weird as right now, watching the two of you kissing. It's like it's indecent or something. Like what you do with each other isn't something anyone else should be watching."

Emma cleared her throat importantly as she sat back down, pushing a plate of warm cookies towards her friend who continued to drink heavily. Alexandra grabbed a cookie and began chewing it.

"What?"

"That's not all of the news the gang was going to share with you tonight."

"No?"

"No."

"Lay it on me. What else?" Alexandra looked sad and thoughtful and not a little drunk as she took another big gulp to wash down the cookie.

"Did you notice Angela hasn't been letting anyone else touch her lately?"

"No, I didn't notice..."

"And José has been pretty much keeping his hands to himself also."

"He was feeling me up pretty good a coupla months ago," Alexandra insisted.

"Yes, in the bar. Not under a table, or out in the car. And a couple of months ago it was different."

"Why?"

Emma smiled at Bob before she spoke, "Angela's pregnant. She and José are getting married too."

"*What?*"

"We were thinking of doing it close together, so we could all celebrate both weddings out here. If that's alright with you..."

Alexandra sat stunned. She stared at first one then the other of her friends, then snapped, "No one tells me anything anymore! I'm only the queen and all, so who cares what I think? No one's asked me what I thought of you all deciding to break up the gang by getting married. Why should you care now? Why should anyone care what I think?"

"Alex, it's not like that," Emma began.

"Alex, we're not breaking up the gang. Some of us are just pairing off. In fact, we owe it all to you."

Emma nodded at Bob as he stopped talking. "That's right, Alex," she continued. "Without you insisting on inviting me to join your gang to meet other men in a non-threatening way after my asshole ex treated me so badly, I've never have met Bob. And since I married so young I was a virgin back then. I didn't know a good lay from a bad lay. Now, thanks to all of the fun we had in your barn, I know what a good lay is. And a great one." She smiled at Bob who leered back at her.

"I guess I'm gonna have to get more guys to join us, huh?" Alexandra spoke as thoughtfully as she could while slightly slurring her words. "Bob's down. José's down. That only leaves six men to keep four women happy. And one of them's me, with my huge appetite for lots of sex."

Emma took a deep breath. "What about Dmitri?"

"Fuck 'im!" Alexandra yelled forcefully. "Fuck 'im! If he doesn't want me, other men do. I'll show that smug Russian son-of-a-bitch who's boss! He thinks he can order me around, huh? I'll show him!"

Alexandra pushed herself up and swayed, holding on to the side of the table for support.

"Are you heading out to the barn?" Bob asked.

"Nah. I'm gonna go soak in the hot tub. Wanna join me?"

"No. I'll just stay and keep Emma company, I think."

Alexandra shrugged and began unlacing her corset.

"Whatever. Suit yourself." She got angry when the laces knotted and stumbled over to a drawer and yanked it open. She pushed stuff around inside of it for a while, mumbling to herself.

"Where's the fucking scissors? I'll just cut the damn thing off...maybe I can use a knife? Emma, you got a sharp knife handy?"

She turned to find Emma holding the scissors. She pushed Alexandra's hands away and carefully cut the knotted laces open. Alexandra massaged the underside of both of her breasts.

"Ah, that's better! Damn thing was so tight I could barely breathe! Hey Bob, you gotta smoke?"

Bob nodded and pulled a pack out of his pocket and lit a cigarette before he passed it to her. Alexandra stuck it into her mouth and grabbed the bottle off the table before heading unsteadily towards the door.

"See ya's later," she said as the door shut behind her.

"Go with her," Emma said quickly to Bob.

"Why?"

"So she doesn't pass out and drown, that's why!"

"What if she gropes me?"

Emma smiled at him. "You're a big boy. You can handle it. Keep your boxers on if you want to. Just think about God and country...or recite baseball statistics in your head. If you don't get hard, she won't try anything."

Bob made a face at her as he sighed heavily. He began to head out the back door but stopped behind her.

"A kiss before I go off to do your bidding, mistress?"

Emma laughed as she pulled his head down and kissed him passionately, ending with licking his chin.

"Now go! Dinner will be ready soon and we've got to get some food into her or she's gonna be really sick tomorrow!"

* * * *

Once the stew was ready, Emma rang the bell outside of the back door to let everyone know, and before too long the kitchen was crowded with nude, hungry bikers. Everyone ate their fill sitting on the back porch, then went back in for seconds. Emma had started an industrial-sized coffeemaker before dinner was served, so by the time everyone started looking for the desserts, the coffee was ready.

Emma and Bob made sure Alexandra had coffee with her cookies and brownies, but that barely slowed down her booze consumption. By the time the campfire had been lit and everyone had found a comfortable chair to sit on, Alexandra was almost done with her second bottle. For the most part she was sitting quietly, as if lost in thought...or too drunk to make words.

When there was a lull in conversation because people were digesting the enormous amount of food they'd consumed, Bob stood up and addressed the crowd.

"I'd like your attention, everyone. You might be wondering why I wasn't out in the barn with the rest of you before dinner. Emma and I have an announcement to make. I've asked and she's accepted, so sometime in the next month she and I are getting married at a courthouse. We'd love for any of you who want to be there as witnesses to come with us, and we're hoping to have a reception of sorts here, to celebrate where we met and fell in love."

There were cheers and congratulations from all sides. The females kissed and groped Bob, telling him it was one last time, for old time's sake! The men were more chaste with their hugs, making sure not to touch any part of Emma that might now be deemed off-limits to anyone other than the groom.

After everyone sat back down, José stood up and cleared his throat.

"Angela and I have an announcement to make also. Over the winter I wasn't as careful as I should have been about using condoms each and every time, so Angela is pregnant. We're also getting married, since that's what you do when this happens."

Angela stuck her tongue out at him. "If that's how you feel, *señor*, then ¡*adios*! The baby and I will do just fine without you!"

José rushed over to kneel in front of her, contrition expressed in his pose.

"¡*Carida! ¡Eres toda mi vida! ¡Te llevo en el alma!*"

Bob laughed. "I think that means he loves her...congratulations, you two!"

More hugging and back-slapping happened, before the two happy couples sat back down. At that point, Alexandra stood up.

"All I gotta say is I don't like change! I didn't like it when my dad dumped my mom for his bimbo. I didn't like it when Mike and Craig left last year, to live other places. And I don't like it that you are pairing off like this! This is supposed to be a gang, not a family gathering! What the fuck? Now, you four will only have sex with each other, right? That leaves less men for the four of us who are too smart to fall in love!"

She sat back down heavily and took another long drink

from what little remained in her bottle. She reached over and plucked a cigarette out of Tom's mouth. He smiled at her before lighting another one.

"We're not being dumb," Emma began. "It's just that none of us expected to meet someone who was so perfect for us there couldn't be any other way for this to end up. Bob is everything I've ever hoped for, but figured after my fucking disaster of a first marriage, I'd never find. I'm just so happy. Please be happy for us, my queen."

Bob patted Emma's hand and nodded, turning to smile at Alexandra.

"After all, we owe meeting and realizing how we felt to you..."

"That's right." Angela bobbed her head in agreement. "I sure wasn't looking to fall in love. I just wanted to have a good time. And look what I found!"

She rubbed her belly that upon close enough inspection did appear to be starting to grow larger. José leaned over and kissed her belly, then his tongue trailed its way up to her lips for a passionate kiss.

"But what about me?" Alexandra wailed.

There was silence for a heartbeat before everyone loudly proclaimed their loyalty to the queen of their gang. Alexandra shook her head and jumped up to yell at everyone.

"I know you're all still here! But he's not! The one guy I want isn't here! Why isn't he here? Why can everyone else find someone to love but I can't?"

In the shocked hush following her outburst, Alexandra burst into tears.

"I want Dmitri! I like his cock! I like the way he treats me! I want him and he left me! He walked out on me!"

Alexandra wavered unsteadily on her feet, as she tilted the bottle up and drained the last of her second bottle of JD for the day. She began to sway, taking a few recovery steps that took her perilously close to the fire. Sensing imminent disaster, two of the men seated close to her rose quickly and reached towards her as she fell heavily. They caught her before she hit the ground or the fire. Her head lolled back as they realized what had happened.

"She's out for the night," Jim said matter-of-factly to Brad.

Emma rose, gesturing towards the house.

"Can you guys get her upstairs? We need to get her into a bed so she can sleep it off."

The two men carried her, one man holding her shoulders, the other her feet. They followed Emma as she led them in through the back door and up the stairs to the second floor where all the bedrooms were. After a few minutes, Jim and Brad returned to the fire and reclaimed their seats.

Emma came out later. As she sat back down on her lawn seat, Bob patted her arm.

"Is she okay?"

Emma nodded. "She passed out. I'll check on her every hour or so, to be sure she's okay. At some point she's gonna be doing some major puking. In the meantime, we have some partying to do, right everyone?"

There was a general grumble of agreement.

"So, who's got the weed?" Emma asked as Bob walked back from the kegger to hand her refilled beer glass to her.

The party went on long into the night. Emma rose a few times to check on their errant queen, but always returned with a smile and a nod for anyone with a question in their eyes.

* * * *

It was quite a few hours later that Emma and Bob groped their way in the dark up the stairs to the door of the room across from Alexandra's. Emma peeked in and by the light of the moon, saw that her friend still slept heavily, snoring in a regular rhythm.

When she rejoined Bob, they fell onto the bed in a paroxysm of passion that expressed how happy they were with each other. They fell asleep entwined in each other's arms.

Emma wasn't sure what woke her up, but she opened her eyes and looked around, noticing the early morning rays of dawn beginning to lighten the room. She rolled to a more comfortable position. The door across the hall creaked.

"Shit! I hope Alex isn't sleep-walking, looking for something to drink! She's probably still drunk. I'd better go be sure she's alright."

She got out of the bed gently, hoping not to disturb Bob who was still asleep.

As she got out into the hall she heard a noise from Alex, slurring her words as she spoke in a low voice.

"Ooh, Dmitri. You did come back...you do love me. Now, fuck me good and hard, like you know I like it."

Surprised, Emma pushed open the door and saw a man in bed behind Alexandra. The early rays of dawn coming through the open windows showed his hands were busy, one twisting a nipple, the other stroking between her legs as she began to writhe against him.

"Who's that? Dmitri, did you come back?" Emma asked.

The man grunted and pushed his hips forward as Alexandra opened her eyes wide in surprise.

"Wha...? Who? That's not the dick I want! Who *is* that?"

The man began to grind against her in earnest as Emma turned on the overhead light.

"Rich! Leave her alone!" Emma yelled so she could be heard over his grunting and Alexandra's protestations.

"Get outta me! I don' wanna fuck you! I...shit! Lemme up... now!"

Realizing what was imminent, Emma yelled, "Get offa her now, Rich! She's gonna..."

With a huge effort, Alexandra rolled over to the side of the bed and began to puke, huge spasms wracking her body as the results of her massive over-indulgence punished her with a vengeance. Rich growled in frustration, attempting to grab her from behind again.

Emma was horrified as she rushed forward to help her friend.

"For fuck's sake, leave her alone! Let her barf in peace, asshole!"

"Who's gonna make me?" Rich glared at her.

"I am." Bob spoke in a loud voice from the doorway as he surveyed the bizarre scene.

Emma held the bulk of Alexandra's hair out of the way as she continued to be wracked by spasms of projectile vomiting, most of which was on the rug next to the bed. Rich tried to edge closer to Alexandra from behind, but her body shook which made her a difficult target to aim into.

"Rich, I'm only going to say this once. Get the fuck out of here and leave her be!" Bob's voice had a dangerous edge to it.

"Why? We've fucked lots of times. What difference does it make if I do her now?"

Bob advanced into the room. "In case you hadn't noticed, she's puking her guts out right now. That's not usually the best kind of foreplay, or during-play for most women. She's not able to give consent because she can't stop barfing long enough to say anything. No woman gets fucked around here unless she wants it."

"You gonna stop me?" Rich growled as he grabbed for her hips again, while she was temporarily quiet in between bouts of nausea.

"Jesus! What the fuck?" Tom entered the room, quickly sizing up what was going on.

Bob explained quickly. "Rich seems to think that now is an excellent time for him to reclaim our queen. She's not really in the mood. I think we should strongly encourage him to leave the room right now."

Tom's face was set in a grim frown as he nodded. "I agree."

"That's two against one, Rich. Should we wake up the other men also, to take a poll? Or are you gonna get your ass up and get out of here? That woman's too sick to want anything to do with any man. You may not be a gentleman, but while I'm here you're not going to be an animal either."

"Fine!" Rich roared in frustration as his feet connected with the floor. He stomped over to the door and pushed at Tom, who didn't move out of the way as quickly as Bob had done.

They heard him still stomping all the way down the stairs, then the kitchen door slammed as he went out into the yard.

Emma was still holding Alexandra's hair. Bob had gone into the bathroom and returned with a cool, wet washcloth, which Emma used to wipe her friend's face.

"Do you think you're done, honey?" She asked solicitously.

Alexandra was too weak to shrug and nodding looked like a huge effort.

"I think so...for now," she answered weakly.

"Okay then." Emma took charge. "Bob, can you get that rug out of here? Put it into a trash bag and seal it closed. Jack smells really bad mixed with food and barf. If she has to keep smelling it, she'll probably keep puking."

"What can I do?" asked Tom.

"Go downstairs and find a can of Coke and a glass. Fill the glass with ice and bring them up here. She needs to hydrate, and water will only make things worse."

Both of the men left the room on their errands.

Emma wiped Alexandra's face, then went out into the hall to the bathroom to rinse the cloth. She returned with two more cool washcloths and a glass of water to use to refresh them. She also had a bottle of pain pills that she set on the nightstand next to the bed, to wait for the iced Coke.

She shook her head as Alexandra moaned, "Kill me now!"

"I'm afraid you're going to have to live through this one, Alex," Emma replied, using the cool cloths to wipe Alex's arms. "You drank two entire bottles of the Reverend Jack yesterday and ate very little. You were trying really hard to get drunk and you did an excellent job of it. You almost passed out in the fire. Lucky for you Jim and Brad caught you, and brought you up here to sleep it off. I checked on you every few hours to be sure you were alright."

"Thanks for taking care of me," Alexandra spoke in a very small voice, as if just talking hurt.

Emma's gentle touch turned rough as she said, "I don't know what the fuck that asshole Rich thought he was doing. I'm just glad I heard the door creak when he found his way up here this morning."

"Ow!"

She was immediately apologetic. "Sorry. I'm just so angry at him right now. I didn't mean to take it out on you."

"I thought it was Dmitri, who'd come back to me..."

"No, Alex. He never came back last night."

Two large tears began to roll down Alexandra's face.

"Maybe he'll never come back. Maybe I've lost him for good."

Emma looked up as Tom returned with the glass of ice and the can of soda, opening it as he walked through the door.

"Anything else I can do?"

Emma shook her head as she poured the Coke into the glass. "No. If you can, try to get back to sleep."

The loud roar of a Harley fired up from the yard as the engine gunned. The bike threw stones and dirt against the side of the house and into the air as it roared out of the yard.

Emma sighed loudly. "That's probably gone and woken everyone up. Tom, maybe you can get some coffee going, in case anyone else can't get back to sleep?"

He nodded, smiling at Alexandra. "I hope you feel better soon."

She bit her lip and nodded, barely holding back the tears that poured out of her the instant he left the room.

Emma held three pills close to Alexandra's mouth. "Here, swallow these. Then drink some Coke. You might not be done barfing yet, but at least it will give you some relief for a while. And you'll have something to puke up besides stomach acid."

Obediently Alexandra swallowed the pills, took a few sips of the soda, then lay back weakly on the pillow, sobbing.

"I don't want to miss him this much. He's just a man. I can get any man I want, so why should I care if he's gone? I can just find another one, right?"

Emma walked over to open the windows wide and let the cool morning breeze into the room to air it out. She pulled a chair over to the side of the bed and sat next to her friend, patting her arm.

"You've always been able to get any man you wanted, Alex. But maybe this one is different. Maybe he wants more than just a piece of you...he wants it all."

"No! No man is ever gonna have that much power over me!"

Suddenly she looked stricken and Emma held out the plastic wastebasket Alexandra had missed completely the first time. Alexandra leaned her face into it and heaved. Emma took the wastebasket from her when she was done and gave her the glass of icy soda again.

"I have a feeling it's going to be a really long recovery for you, Alex," she said.

"You mean from my hangover?"

Emma nodded, "Yeah, that...and if Dmitri really is done with you. I think you've gone and fallen for him. You just have to decide if you are going to go after him or let him walk away."

Alexandra lay back on the pillow once again and moaned. Emma pulled the sheet up over her, so she wouldn't get chilled. She rinsed the cloths in the bathroom sink and returned to place them on Alexandra's forehead and arms. She was silent for so long, Emma leaned over to check. Satisfied her queen had fallen asleep, she quietly moved out of the room to go downstairs and see about feeding the rest of the people she'd heard moving around.

Chapter Eleven

Sunday's ride back home to Minneapolis was brutal. Still not fully recovered, Alexandra had to fight her stomach not to heave while she was on the road. Once she reached her condo, she took a long shower and went to bed. She slept so long that she got up an hour earlier than usual in the morning, and had time to make herself a light breakfast of toast and fruit, along with the one cup of coffee she was able to drink.

By Wednesday her body had totally healed itself, but her emotions were still in an upheaval. After she ate the dinner she had picked up on the way home, she kept her phone nearby as she worked out, trying to sweat out any of the poisons she might not have expelled while recovering. The phone never did anything to indicate a call or a text.

After she'd exhausted herself, she finished the bottle of water nearby, frowned and stared moodily at the offending phone in her hand.

"You're waiting for me to make the first move, aren't you?" She said aloud to the phone, but really to the man she had thought about constantly over the past few days. "Okay, then I will..."

She found his number and hit call, then immediately cancelled the call.

"Shit! I don't have any idea what to say. *Come on over and fuck me hard, big guy?* Then he's gonna want to know if I'm ready to give up other men for him. Am I? Fucked if I know. Can't he just come over and hold me, while I think about it? God, I sound so needy. What's happening to me? I don't like feeling like this, but I don't seem to be able to do anything about it."

A text? Yeah, that's safer. No emotions in a text. I can make it seem like I don't care if he comes over or not, I was just wondering if I should expect him...

Satisfied she had a solution, she began to compose her message.

R U coming over 2nite? She hit *send*.

While she waited for a response, she went into the kitchen and got another bottle of water. She still felt dehydrated and the work-out had made things worse. She almost ran back to the phone when she heard the beep to indicate she had a text. Her hand shook while she held up the phone and looked at the return text from Dmitri.

Can't. In Chicago again. Same business. She was glad she hadn't called, because against her will, tears formed in her eyes and her throat hurt from the sudden urge to give in to her continuing disappointment.

Will U B back by Friday? She took deep breaths after hitting *send* again, trying to control the emotions that sabotaged her efforts to be cool and collected.

Not sure. Maybe.

U know where I'll B. She paused and added, *I miss U.*

The tears suddenly flowed down her face as she blinked at them, watching the screen for his reply. It never came.

She walked into her bedroom and carefully placed the phone next to her bed on the nightstand. She waited a moment in case he replied. Maybe he was busy, or driving or... something. She went into the bathroom for a shower. Once the water soothed her overly-wound muscles, she stopped fighting her tears and cried all through her shower.

He hates me! He's not coming back to me. He's probably got another woman in Chicago. Business my ass! I've lost him and it's my own damn fault. I didn't even know how much I wanted him and now he's gone. What good does it do me to tell him I need other men too, when he's all the man I really want?

When she crept into bed and curled into a fetal ball, her thoughts brought little comfort.

This is what it feels like to be in love? It sucks! It fucking hurts. Nothing will ever be the same for me. I've always been the one to end things...the one to walk away. The one in charge. Now? Now I'm just like any other love-struck female. I'm disgusted with myself. I'm embarrassed. And I'm in pain. And I won't have any idea how to act if I ever see him again. I'll want to throw myself on him and beg him not to ever leave me again. What if he laughs at me? What if he has already found someone else? I hate my life!

Her last thought added guilt to every other depressing feeling she experienced.

Mom? I'm so sorry I always judged you...always told you that you were a fool for still loving Dad. I'm sorry, Mom!

For the next few days, what little sleep she did get was fitful.

* * * *

Friday night came and still Dmitri didn't show up or call. Determined to carry on as if her heart wasn't breaking daily, she changed into her leathers and jeans, and rode to the hangout bar. Everyone was happy to see her, if tentative about mentioning the past weekend. She dealt with that by joking about it.

"Yeah, I'll have another beer. Shit yeah! Just don't anybody offer me any shots of Reverend Jack! I've had it with that guy for a while...we're not on friendly terms anymore."

Everyone laughed then and Alexandra was almost happy. But then she looked around for someone to dance with when her favorite song came on, and realized that the one man she really wanted to hold in her arms wasn't there. She felt her unhappiness drown her in its depths. She chugged the last of the beer in her glass and headed for the pool table, thinking that beating the new guys playing there might lift her mood. And temporarily, it did.

A few hours later she looked up as Tom touched her arm.

"Need anything from the gas station across the street, my queen?"

She smiled at him, shaking her head. "Are you out of smokes again? You always run out! Haven't you learned yet that you always smoke more than a pack when you're here? I'll bet they cost more over there..."

He shook his head, grinning, "Nah. That's the best part. They sell 'em discounted. So I tell myself I won't smoke more than a pack, then when I have to run across the street to get more, at least I can get them real cheap. I'll be back in a few minutes."

He leaned over and gave her a quick kiss on her lips, and made his way through the throng of Friday-night-partying bikers to disappear through the door.

Alexandra had just poured herself more beer from the fresh pitcher when the front door was flung open and a man yelled into the crowded bar, "Someone call 9-1-1! My fucking phone's dead! There's been an accident out front! Jesus Christ! I think he's dead!"

The bartender dialed the bar phone while people rushed for the front door. Alexandra looked around and realized Tom hadn't returned yet. She had a very bad feeling about what was out the door, in the street. She tried to force her way through the crowd, and was only partially successful. By the time she got outside and could see the body, the ambulance sirens were already screaming on their way to the scene. The police car skidded to a stop right in front of her, cutting off her view, but she'd already seen what she was afraid she'd see.

She pushed her way through the crowd and around the car, closer to the body as the ambulance arrived. Emma knelt on the ground, holding Tom's hand, using her other hand to smooth his hair across his forehead, the same way she had soothed Alexandra. Bob was right behind her, awkwardly patting her on the shoulder, as if passing his strength to her so she could pass it to Tom.

Alexandra fell to her knees next to Emma. "Is he…"

Emma shook her head sadly. Alexandra took his hand in hers and he opened his eyes slightly, trying to focus on her face.

"Hush, Tom, I'm here," she said.

"My queen?" He coughed, dark red blood pouring from his mouth.

"I told you smoking wasn't good for you…" She felt tears streaming down her face as he tried to grin at her.

"Better give it up, then…"

His eyes rolled back in his head and the lids closed. The EMTs knelt next to him on the opposite side and began to check his vital signs. Bob used a hand on each of their shoulders to get them both to stand up, so they would be out of the way of the med-techs who needed space to do their jobs.

They watched as a stretcher was placed next to him and he was eased onto it, then carried to the ambulance. The door slammed shut and the sirens were turned back on as it screamed out its urgency and careened into the night. The police began to question everyone who was around, looking for someone who might have witnessed the hit-and-run accident.

The man who had initially run into the bar had been walking his dog past the bar when he heard a car revving its motor before the tires screamed and it raced down the street. He'd looked up in time to see the body being tossed through the air.

"I'll never forget the sound it made when he hit the street. Sounded like every bone in his body was broken all at once! It was terrible!"

Amid his shocked ramblings, what became clear was that the only thing he could remember about the car was that it was a black, mid-sized sedan. It drove away too fast and he didn't have his glasses on, so he didn't see the license plates at all. And he never saw the driver.

Once the police had cleared Alexandra, Emma and Bob, they asked which hospital the ambulance had gone to, and they raced to their bikes to follow it. They parked in the emergency lot and strode quickly into the lobby of the ER. They had to talk fast to convince the nurses they really knew Tom, but fortunately soon after their arrival, one of the policemen who was asking questions at the scene, walked in and affirmed their connection. They sat on one side of the room, quietly sipping coffee from the machine in the lobby. The policeman sat on the other side, his walkie-talkie occasionally squawking out unintelligible noises.

None of them had ever met any of Tom's family, so when his mother came in, accompanied by a younger version of Tom, they were hesitant about introducing themselves. The older woman and the young man sat down across from them and Alexandra nodded to them, initiating conversation.

"I'm Alex. Tom has ridden with my gang for almost a year. He's a good man."

The older woman choked back a sob and nodded. "Thanks."

The young man asked, "Do you know what happened?"

They shared what they knew, which wasn't much. Bob asked, then got both of them a cup of coffee and they resumed their silent vigil.

Alexandra had just gotten another cup of coffee and sat back down on one side of Bob, so he could put an arm around her, as he had his other arm around Emma. A doctor walked slowly into the waiting area and looked around for the policeman, who jumped up to conference with him. Their words were too quiet for anyone to hear, but when the policeman turned to face them, they all knew what he was going to say.

"I'm sorry, he didn't make it."

"No!" The woman sobbed, standing up to grab at the doctor, before collapsing into her chair. Her son rubbed her back, attempting to soothe her as he listened to the doctor's words.

"He suffered too much internal damage and went into cardiac arrest while we were trying to stabilize him."

"Can we see him? To say goodbye?" The young man's face was ashen as he assumed the role of protecting his mother, yet insisting on closure for both of them.

"Of course. Follow me." The doctor led them through the door he had come out of. They never looked back.

The policeman cleared his throat. "There's no reason for the rest of you to stay here any longer. You'll be contacted by a detective, probably tomorrow. If there's anyone you can think of who might have wanted to harm this guy..."

"His name was Tom. Tom Taylor."

The policeman stared at Alexandra as he spoke. "Yes. If you can think of anyone who wanted to harm Tom Taylor, you'll be given an opportunity to share that information when you are contacted. Don't leave town."

Alexandra turned to see Emma sobbing in Bob's arms. He looked up and saw the look on her face. He held out an arm and Alexandra joined them in a group embrace, tears running down her face.

Outside in the cool night, Emma turned to Alexandra as she got onto her bike.

"If you don't want to be alone tonight, you can stay with us. We have a guest room or you can sleep on the sofa in the living room..."

Alexandra looked at them both as Bob managed an encouraging smile and nod. For an instant she thought of how unfair it was that she had to be alone...that everyone else had someone to be with, but not her. Then she remembered that was her choice and she shook her head slowly.

"No." She spoke so quietly it was almost a whisper. "I'll be fine. You two go on home."

"Text me when you get home so we know you're alright, okay?" Emma patted her arm as she spoke.

Alexandra nodded. "I will."

She turned the key and started her bike. She didn't remember any of the ride home, but when she got there, after she texted Emma, she called Dmitri. He didn't answer, so she left a message.

"Dmitri? I know it's late, but I just got home from the hospital. Tom was hit by a car tonight...a hit-and-run. He's dead. I don't know when the wake or funeral will be, but I feel dead inside. I miss you. I want..." Her voice broke. She took a deep, staggered breath and continued.

"I want to feel your arms around me, so I can spend just a few minutes thinking that things are going to be alright. I hope you'll be back soon."

* * * *

Dmitri was asleep when she called. He didn't hear his phone because the battery had died and he hadn't noticed. But when he woke up in the morning, he checked it and finding it dead, he plugged it in. As soon as it had enough power to beep, it indicated he had voicemail. He only listened to it once, but that was enough. He began making some calls.

* * * *

On Saturday morning, Alexandra was awoken by the insistent sound of her phone. It wasn't the ring-tone she used for her dad, so she almost didn't bother answering. Then she thought better of it.

It might be Dmitri!

She grabbed the phone off the nightstand and mumbled, "Hello?"

"Good morning, Miss Blackstone. This is Detective Mark Jones. I've been assigned to investigate the hit and run accident that resulted in the death of a..."There was a pause as if he was checking his notes. "...a Mister Tom Taylor. Your name was given to me as one of the witnesses. I'd like to ask you a few questions. Can you come around to the station this morning?"

Sitting up, Alexandra spoke, "Of course. Tell me which station it is and I'll be there in an hour."

"Excellent."

After getting directions from the detective, Alexandra got up, showered and dressed. She took her SUV to the station, stopping along the way to pick up coffee for herself and a dozen donuts to share with the detectives on duty.

Doesn't hurt to come bearing gifts, right? Everyone knows policemen love donuts. Besides, I need to eat something. My stomach is empty and my emotions feel raw. Maybe a blast of sugar will help.

In the noise and confusion of the station, Alexandra felt anxious and overwhelmed. Even sitting and answering the questions the detective asked was difficult, since she had trouble shutting out the other voices all around her.

"For the records, Miss, since I'm taping your responses, what is your name?"

"I'm Alexandra Blackstone."

"What was your relationship with Tom Taylor?"

"It's my biker gang Tom rode with for the past year or so."

"Do you ride together every night?"

"No, I don't ride on weekdays...only on weekends. It's how I relax from my very busy job running a marketing firm my father founded."

"Were you very close to Tom?"

"Yes, I'd say we were probably Tom's closest friends. He spent most Friday and Saturday nights with us. We rode together every weekend it was possible to take our Harleys on the road."

"Do you just ride aimlessly, or do you have a particular place you ride to?"

"We have a destination most weekends. It's a place up by Mille Lacs. It's a farm of about ten acres that has been in my family for a long time. No one else ever goes there, so I've been paying the taxes on it for years. Everyone thinks of it as my place. It's a nice ride up there, and we can party without disturbing anyone if we have campfires late into the night."

Alexandra began to shift around on her chair, partly out of nerves, but partly out of irritation at the inevitability of the next question.

"Is your gang involved with anything illegal, like drugs?"

"No, we don't deal drugs. We're not that kind of gang. Yes, we have kegs and cases of booze, but no drugs up at my place when we're there."

The detective's eyebrows rose as if he doubted her response.

"Honestly, sir, I can't afford that kind of scandal to be attached to my name. That would have a deleterious effect on my reputation, and that I can't allow."

"Does your father know about what you do with your spare time?"

"No, my father doesn't know anything about my gang. He bought me my first Harley when I was in college so he knows I ride. But he prefers not to know anything else about that part of my life."

She shifted around impatiently.

"Honestly, I don't see what any of this has to do with your investigation into the accident that killed Tom."

The detective cleared his throat importantly. "We're trying to figure out if it *was* an accident. If it was, we'll continue to try to locate the driver but without any eye-witnesses, that will slow things down. If there's any indication that this was a purposeful death, then we need to follow up with any leads we can discover."

Alexandra leaned forward. "Purposeful death? You mean murder?"

The detective nodded.

"No one would murder Tom! He didn't have an enemy in the world. He was a totally nice guy who made friends wherever he went. No one ever fought with him because he wouldn't rise to any bait. When we'd get in bar fights just for fun, he'd usually just sit it out, watching. He'd help any of us who got hurt, but he didn't like to fight. I can't believe you think anyone had any kind of grudge against such a nice young man."

The detective's eyebrows rose again at her words.

"He was quite a bit younger than you, wasn't he?"

Alexandra exploded. "What the fuck does that have to do with anything? Yeah, I'm thirty-five and he was twenty-six. Way too young to be dead, for sure. Why aren't you out trying to find a car with damage or something, instead of pestering me about how old I am?"

A semblance of a grin flitted across the man's face then he gazed at her steadily.

"We are doing just that, Miss Blackstone and we are interviewing everyone who was at the bar that night."

"Well, duh. If we were *at* the bar that night, then we had nothing to do with it, right? Kind of hard to drive a car out front while you're sitting at the bar drinking."

He nodded. "Yes, I think I'm done with questioning you for now but until this investigation is closed, don't leave town."

"Does that mean I can't go up to my place by Mille Lac?"

"Give me the address and we'll add it to your file."

After she did, the detective rose to shake her hand. He didn't grimace when she clasped his hand firmly, but a flicker of surprise raced through his eyes.

Yeah, that's right, old man. I know how to shake hands as well as you do! I may not be a man, but there're some things my father made sure I could do as well as a man. So there, Fucker!

Alexandra smiled sweetly. "So, are we done, Detective Jones?"

He nodded. "For now."

"Then have a nice day."

Alexandra made sure to put some extra swing into her hips as she sashayed out of the station. She knew she wasn't imagining the hush that accompanied her deliberate bump and grind as she walked through a station of mostly men.

Take that, you assholes! Find who killed Tom and leave me the fuck alone!

When she got back to her condo, she decided she needed a ride to clear her mind. She quickly changed into her jeans, an athletic bra and a leather vest. She tied her hair back and jammed her sunglasses on her face. Once she was on her bike, she rode with no destination in mind, just for the feel of the air as it rushed past her face. She chased all thoughts from her mind to concentrate on the feel of the road. It worked its usual magic on her and for a few short hours, she wasn't upset or depressed…just empty.

When she got back from her ride, Alexandra decided she needed to work out her frustrations with exercise. She ran on her treadmill until she was bathed in sweat. She lay on her bench and lifted weights until her arms burned. She did sit-ups until her stomach hurt and leg-lifts until her legs cramped up. Then she filled her Jacuzzi with scented oil and settled into a very hot bath.

Aah, she thought as she sunk down into the water, the bubbling water tickling her nose. *The trick is not to think. Just to feel. Not to feel emotions, just to feel the pains in my body from over-use. Now I'll feel the muscles relaxing from the hot water.* She leaned back and concentrated on consciously breathing deeply, in and out…in and out.

* * * *

Dmitri had spent the day changing his travel plans. As he made his way back to the big, busty red-head who had so captivated his every thought, he pondered what it was about her he found so attractive.

I love to fuck her. That's a given. She's the hottest, most responsive female I've ever had the pleasure to enjoy. Every little touch makes her quiver, which makes her pussy tighten until I can't control myself anymore. She's a fucking wildcat in bed!

He shifted around in his seat, trying not to make it obvious he was adjusting himself away from the zipper digging into his throbbing flesh.

But she's also a very smart woman. No one can put anything over on her. She plays with the big boys in a man's business and she's extremely successful.

She can wheel and deal, and beat them all at their own game. Then she counts her money, laughing all the way to the bank. She looks so damn good in a suit that the men she's dealing with don't know where to look. I'm sure part of her success is because some of the blood that should be in their brains helping them make decisions, is in their dicks making them wonder what it would be like to fuck her on her desk... like I did the first time I met her.

He smiled, the memories washing over him in waves of remembered pleasure.

And when she's in her biker queen mood? Jesus! Just remembering those huge tits in a black leather bra almost makes me come! She can out-drink, out-party and out-ride most men. But when she's ready to get down to business, I want it to be with me...not the other guys in her gang.

Shit! I thought I was just hanging around for a little fun... trying to tame her just to prove I could. I've gone and fallen hard for that red-haired wildcat. I can't imagine wanting any other woman anymore. I don't know how she feels yet, but she misses me and that's a good sign. I just hope she misses me enough to give up fucking other men. I won't share her...I can't. She's got to belong to me. That's the way it has to be.

When he entered her condo, Dmitri looked around for her. Not hearing anything, he walked down the hallway. He peaked into the kitchen, then smiled at his own foolishness.

She never spends any time in there! I'll just check the bedroom. If she's not home, I'll go pick up some extra food for a couple of days, then I'll come back and wait for her.

The bedroom was empty, but there was a towel discarded on the floor next to the weight bench and empty water bottles strewn around.

She's been working out recently...apparently with a vengeance. She's trying really hard to not think about what's happening.

As he stood there quietly, his brain made sense out of the humming noise he could hear coming from the bathroom.

She's soaking in the Jacuzzi.

His cock twitched in response to imagining her naked and covered with water. He strode over to the bathroom and turned the handle to open the door.

Alexandra had piled her hair on top of her head and held it in place with a clip. Errant tendrils framed her face and trailed around her in the bubbling water. Her breasts floated in front of her, rising into view and falling below the water as she breathed deeply. Since her eyes were closed, Dmitri allowed himself a few moments to admire her, his eyes drinking in the sight of the woman who dominated his every fantasy, his every waking thought. He sucked in a breath and stared.

Jesus, woman! You own me! I'm giving you this kind of power over me. And I'm glad of it! Oh God, please let her be feeling the same way! I won't ask for anything else...ever.

He cleared his throat, but the lack of response from the woman let him know the sound of the Jacuzzi bubbling was too loud for her to notice him. He spoke louder than usual, so she would hear him.

"Alexandra? I'm back."

She opened her eyes and stared at him for a heartbeat. Then she leaned over and turned off the bubbles which made the room eerily quiet. Quickly she rose from the water and held out her arms to him. His brain went into over-drive as it took in the sight of her naked flesh, dripping wet from the bath, shiny from the scented oil, and inviting him to touch it. He went to her without a word and pulled her into his arms.

The angle was awkward because he was out of the tub and she was still in it. But he held her close, his hands roaming on her skin, his nose buried in her hair. Gradually he became aware she was trembling, and the sound he was hearing was her sobbing as if her heart was broken.

I'm such a pig! She's in pain and all I can think about is how much I want to be plunging into her hotness. No! I want to be all the man she needs. I have to prove that to her right now.

"Oh God, *Sashka*, don't cry, dear heart. I'm here. I won't leave you again."

Her shaking only got worse, so Dmitri did the only thing he could think of. He picked her up out of the water and carried her in his arms, through the bathroom door, and over to the bed. He sat on it and held her on his lap, rocking gently to soothe her. He murmured comforting words to her in Russian, heedless of the fact she wouldn't understand a word he said. But she must know how he felt. She must know he would gladly suffer any pain with her, do anything, in order to make things right for her.

Gradually she stopped shaking and her sobs grew quieter. Eventually she was quiet in his arms. With great effort, he ignored the insistent bulge in his pants that kept reminding him she was still wet, still naked, still in his arms...on his lap. And that it had been almost two weeks since they had last made love.

She twined an arm up to caress the hair on the back of his head and neck. As she did, she tilted her head back to look up into his face. They gazed into each other's eyes for a long moment. When Dmitri finally spoke, his voice sounded so unlike his usual gruff tone, even he was surprised. Her eyebrows rose.

"I'm guessing it's been a very long time since you've cried, *Sashka*?"

She nodded slowly. "Yes."

"Or accepted comfort from anyone for your pain?"

"Yes." Her voice sounded unusually soft also.

Dmitri took a deep breath. "I want to be here when you need me, *Sashka*. I want to lessen your pain by sharing it with you and I want to celebrate your joys with you. I want to be all the man you need."

"You do, don't you?" Her eyes reflected wonder.

He nodded.

She reached a hand further up onto the back of his head and pulled him down so she could touch her lips to his.

Steady! Keep yourself together! Don't attack her while she's still fragile.

Obviously Alexandra didn't realize she was still fragile. Her other arm moved up and she plastered her naked breasts against Dmitri's chest as her kiss gained in intensity. Her lips pressed against his harder and she began to moan. She licked at his lips and he opened his mouth in surprise, only to have her push her tongue in to duel with his.

Dmitri was so busy responding to her he didn't notice she'd slid off of his lap to sit on the bed until she pulled him down to lie on top of her. Then all thinking became impossible as they tore at his clothing, both of them intent on getting him naked as soon as possible.

Alexandra slipped his T-shirt up, licking and biting at his nipples, while her hands worked on his zipper. Dmitri reared up and pulled off his shirt, then rolled onto his back to finish pulling his pants down his hips, tossing them onto the floor.

When he looked back over at Alexandra, her hands pushed the sides of her breasts together to make spectacular cleavage he had to dive into. He fastened his mouth onto the nipple closest to him and sucked it in, clamping his lips down on it and teasing the tip in his mouth with his tongue. Alexandra moaned as he reached his hand over to cup the other breast in his palm, then his fingers pinched and rolled the other nipple.

Her hands traced along his sides down to his hips, where one hand sought for and enclosed the pulsating prick that wept with joy at her attention. It was Dmitri's turn to moan as he allowed Alexandra to pull him on top of her. He positioned himself between her legs and pushed into her. It took all his strength to resist the urge to plunge himself deeply into her all at once.

"Yes!" She hissed as her body stretched to accommodate him. "That's what I've needed! That's what I want! I want you, Dmitri! Just you!"

Hearing what he had wanted her to say for so long made him crazy and he forgot he was trying to be gentle. His hands gripped her hips and he shoved himself forward forcefully. Fearing he was hurting her, he looked up at her face. Her eyes were closed tightly and her mouth was open in a huge smile as she shrieked.

"Yes! Oh yes! That's what I need! That's what I've been missing! Ride me hard, Dmitri! Ride me until I can't feel anything except you! Until I can't think of anything but you! Until all there is for me is you! You and..." She panted. "Just a little bit over to this side...you sweet mother-fucking miracle-man! Dmitre-ee-ee-ah!"

She pushed over the edge to tremble with the intensity of the orgasms that wracked her body. Her arms were stretched out to the side and her nails tore at the sheets as she reared up off the bed. She screamed as her inner walls pulsated and squeezed. Dmitri had no choice but to pull her close one last time, their pelvises glued tightly together as he felt himself lose control to the intense spasms that reached deep into his soul and milked the burning fluids out of him...the ultimate act of claiming the woman for himself, marking her as his. He roared out his pleasure as they bucked against each other, each lost in their own bliss, yet each aware of the connection between their bodies.

With a final groan, Dmitri collapsed forward, unable to hold himself up anymore. Alexandra screamed one last time then was silent. Her blood was pounding so fast, Dmitri could watch her pulse beating against the skin of her neck. He opened his mouth and licked at her pulse, tasting the saltiness of her sweat along with what his tongue recognized as his favorite flavor of woman. With a massive effort, Dmitri rolled over onto his back, pulling her with him.

Alexandra giggled. "How can you still be hard enough to be inside of me after an orgasm like that?"

Dmitri shrugged, the movement making her head bounce on his chest.

"See what you do to me? I don't need any recovery time with you. I want you again as soon as we're done."

He twitched consciously, to prove his words. She responded by squeezing him tightly, then releasing until he grew even harder.

"God," Alexandra panted, "I've missed having you in my bed. I've missed your arms holding me. We need to make up for lost time."

They spent some time doing just that, rediscovering just how much they both enjoyed each other. Much later, after they had eaten the pizza they had delivered and finished a chilled bottle of her favorite Italian sparkling wine, they soaked for a short time in the Jacuzzi. They relaxed against their respective sides of the tub until they felt waterlogged. They retired to the bedroom to once again express their unmitigated joy at being together.

Afterwards, Dmitri returned from the bathroom to find Alexandra lying on her stomach, smiling at him as he walked back to the bed.

"Now that's a sight I've been seeing in all of my dreams lately," she began.

"What?"

"You walking naked back to my bed."

Dmitri smiled as he climbed onto the bed and moved closer to her. "Do you want a back-rub? You've been under a huge amount of pressure lately. I'm offering my services, my lady."

Alexandra patted his thigh. "As long as you don't get upset if I fall asleep. I haven't been getting much sleep lately, and it's been filled with nightmares and anxiety dreams. Having you next to me will hopefully allow me to relax enough to actually get a good night's rest."

Dmitri positioned himself almost sitting on her upper thighs as he began to massage her shoulders.

"Wow, you weren't kidding. Your shoulders are knotted. It's going to take me a while to get these muscles to relax. You just lie there and enjoy while I work them."

His fingers massaged the shoulder muscles until they softened a bit, then he traveled down her back, then back up along the spine. On his second time on her shoulders, he was rewarded by feeling them relaxing more easily. But he was amused when her entire body twitched suddenly.

"Am I hurting you, *Sashka*?"

No answer. He leaned over to inhale the scent of her hair once again, and heard a quiet snore.

"Ah, you have fallen asleep, my love. Good. Rest easy, knowing your man is here and I will slay any dragons that might attempt to disturb you."

He rolled over to her side and pulled her closer into his arms. He buried his nose in her hair and breathed in deeply.

And I will rest easy knowing you are finally realizing you don't need anyone else except me. A hard-won victory, but one I will cherish forever. My Sashka.

Chapter Twelve

Alexandra's eyes popped open on Sunday morning and she sniffed the air, certain the intoxicating smell of bacon was what had woken her up. She stretched luxuriously, every part of her body feeling relaxed and comfortable. She knew without looking Dmitri had already risen, so after she visited the bathroom she padded down the hall, following the smell of food, to look for him.

She found Dmitri bent over to put a pan in the oven. Alexandra let out a wolf whistle. He shut the oven door and turned to smile at her.

"Was that for me, Ma'am?"

"Why, yes it was, Mister. That's one fine-looking ass you have there, on display for me. But one question: aren't you afraid to fry bacon *au naturale*? I mean those tiny splatters of grease could really hurt some delicate areas."

Dmitri grinned wider. "Thanks for your concern. But I cooked the bacon in the oven while I got everything else ready. I ran out earlier while you were still getting your beauty sleep and I picked up some food for today."

"I presume you had to put on clothes to do that?"

"Of course, but I stripped as soon as I got back, then got to cooking. I was going to come in soon to wake you with a cup of coffee, and we would have some time to enjoy each other before the *strata* is ready."

"Oh? My bad! Forget you saw me at all. I'm really still in bed, awaiting my morning coffee."

She turned and walked quickly down the hall to hurl herself onto the bed. She pulled the sheet up and over her breasts and lay back on the pillow, pretending to be asleep.

A few minutes later, Dmitri entered the room with the coffeepot, two cups, and a small bottle of cream for her coffee. He placed everything on the nightstand next to the bed and poured coffee into both cups before crawling onto the bed to nuzzle Alexandra's neck.

"Your coffee has arrived, *Sashka* and we have about forty-five minutes to amuse ourselves. Whatever shall we do with the time?"

She reached up both arms and pulled him on top of her, her hands roaming down to massage his butt cheeks as she writhed under him. In response he moved against her, feeling himself aching with desire for the woman he never seemed to be able to get enough of.

They made good use of the time they had, then enjoyed breakfast sitting naked out on the balcony terrace outside her bedroom. They toasted each other with mimosas and coffee, and enjoyed the sunshine that streamed over them.

The rest of the day was just as spectacular. Dmitri had bought dinner supplies and he grilled pork tenderloin Russian-style, which they enjoyed with grilled potatoes and a fresh beet salad with blue cheese. They never bothered to put on any clothing and simply enjoyed being with each other.

* * * *

It was with great difficulty that Alexandra forced herself to go to work on Monday morning and Dmitri drove off to continue working on the mysterious business he had referred to a few times.

Alexandra was busy doing research for a new client when her phone rang.

"Hello?"

"Is this Alexandra Blackstone?" The voice sounded vaguely familiar.

"Yes. You called me at work, so you must have known that. What can I do for you?"

"This is Detective Mark Jones again, Miss Blackstone. I would like for you to stop by the station this morning, if you can work it into your schedule."

"What is this about, Detective? Do you have any news about the hit and run driver who killed Tom?"

The Detective cleared his throat. "Ahem...I'd rather speak to you in my office, if you don't mind."

"Well I do mind because I have a pretty busy day going here, Detective."

"When do you take your lunch break?"

Alexandra sighed. "Usually at one, when my secretary is

done with hers. Oh, very well. I'll be there shortly after one. Is it alright with you if I bring my lunch with me?"

"By all means. I often eat at my desk, so it won't be the first time food has been around here. See you then, Miss Blackstone."

Somehow Alexandra kept her mind on her work enough to get some things accomplished before she took a late lunch at 1:30. Then she remembered she needed to eat in the police station. She went through the drive-through window of her favorite local sub sandwich place, then strode into the station on a mission: eat her lunch and get the detective to leave her alone at work.

The man was on the phone as she approached his desk, so she walked up to take the seat she'd been in before. She put her bottle of water on the desk and the bag of food next to it, then carefully unwrapped her sandwich and began to eat. He gave her a grim smile, but continued his conversation. She spent the time looking around at the busy, noisy and unpleasant surroundings and silently thanked her dad for being a businessman who wanted her to follow in his footsteps, not a cop.

"Later," the detective said, clicking his phone off and turning to look at her.

"Thank you for your time, Miss Blackstone. I know you are a busy woman."

"Yes, I am. So get to the point. Why did you need to talk to me here?"

"Did you know a man named Jim Richmond?"

"Yes, of course I know...wait, you said *did*, didn't you? Why?"

"Because he was found on the street in front of a store he regularly serviced on Saturday afternoons. Apparently he was the victim of a drive-by shooting, but we haven't been able to find any eye-witnesses yet."

Alexandra stopped chewing to stare in disbelief at the officer.

"He was shot? Is he...?"

He shook his head. "He was declared DOA by the emergency room when they got him there. His customer had gone into the store carrying the first load of groceries he was delivering, and when he got back out into the street he found Jim's body next to his truck."

Alexandra sat in stunned silence for a few minutes before a tear rolled down her face.

The detective cleared his throat. "So I take it he was one of your gang of motorcycle riders?"

Alexandra nodded, still dazed.

"How long have you known him?"

"He's been riding with me for about five years...almost as long as I've called my friends who ride with me on weekends, my *gang*."

The detective offered her a box of tissues, but Alexandra used one of the napkins on her lap to wipe her eyes.

"I'm sorry to have to ask you this again, but do you know anyone who might have wanted Jim Richmond dead? Did he have any enemies? Was he in any fights or arguments lately?"

Alexandra let out a snort that ended in a sob.

"Jim? When *wasn't* he getting himself into fights and arguments? He was just that kind of guy. He liked to spar and he liked to fight. But in a clincher, he's the one you want guarding your back. He'll make sure you're okay and the other guy is the one sent to the hospital. That's the kind of man Jim was."

She sat silently for a few moments, wiping her eyes before she blew her nose.

"Wait a minute. You're asking me the same questions you asked about Tom. You don't think their deaths were random accidents?"

Detective Jones stared at her intently, as if watching her every reaction.

"I'm not sure what to think yet, at this point. But it does seem odd that two men who were known to you...who were a part of a weekend motorcycle gang with you, were killed within twenty-four hours of each other."

Alexandra took a long drink from her water bottle, ignoring her discarded sandwich.

"Do you have any suspects?"

"No. That's why I wanted to ask you first. You're the leader of this gang. I figured that if anyone knew of enemies of these guys, it would be you."

Alexandra shook her head slowly.

"Can you tell me where you were Saturday afternoon, Miss Blackstone?"

Her eyes opened wide as she shook her head.

"Um...no. I was freaked out after I talked with you here,

so I went home and changed into my riding gear, then I hit the road. I rode for hours, with no destination in mind. I just wanted to feel the road and the wind in my face."

"I did ask you not to leave town, if you will remember..."

"But I wasn't leaving town. I was just riding to empty my head of bad unpleasant thoughts."

"I see. Was anyone else riding with you?"

"No. The whole point was to get away from everything and everyone. So I was alone. There were no witnesses, unless you can find some of the guys who whistled at me as I rode by them, or the truckers who kept blowing their horns and yelling obscene invitations at me to meet them at the next truck-stop."

The man's lips curled upwards then he quickly rearranged his face back to its solemn neutrality.

"I'm sure anyone on the road would remember *you* riding by. If we need to find witnesses, we'll check some trucker companies for driving records."

"But you have no other clues or leads to go on?"

"Not yet. But we're working on it."

Alexandra looked at her forgotten sandwich with distaste. She re-wrapped it and stuffed it into the bag it had come in, then she rose.

"Are we done here? I do have a job I need to get back to."

Detective Jones rose also. "Yes, we're done...for now. But like I said before, don't leave town."

"You'll call me if you find out anything?"

"I'll call you if I have any more questions, from any of the leads we are following up on."

Alexandra grimaced. "Not the same thing, but it'll have to do. Good-bye, Detective Jones. Nothing personal, but I hope I don't see you again very soon."

He nodded. "I understand. Good-bye, Miss Blackstone."

This time Alexandra felt too defeated to swing her hips around on the way out the door. Her thoughts were like squirrels running loose in her head.

Losing two of my closest friends to random violence so close together is bad enough. But the idea that someone might have killed them on purpose is beyond unsettling. What kind of twisted fuck would kill sweet, innocent Tom?

She had trouble concentrating on her job for the rest of the afternoon. It wasn't helped by the knowledge she had to head to the wake for Tom after she left her office. She had purposely worn a dark suit for that reason.

She parked her SUV in the ample lot at the funeral home. She looked around and recognized the bikes there, so at least she'd have friends to talk to, instead of having to spend all of her time making awkward yet polite conversation with Tom's mother and brother.

Hell, they might blame me for this. After all, if Tom hadn't joined my gang, this might not have happened! I wish this was a nightmare so I could wake up.

She took a deep breath and pushed open the door. She looked around and saw an officious man heading towards her. He was dressed like any other funeral director she'd ever seen, in a conservative, tailored dark suit. He'd been talking to some people spilling out of one of the chapels, but obviously wanted to be the one to direct her himself.

"Can I help you, Miss?" He asked with an unctuous smile.

"I'm looking for the wake for Tom Taylor."

"He's in the smaller chapel in the back. I could take you there..."

She shook her head. "That won't be necessary. I'm sure I can find it. In fact I see someone I know now. Thanks."

Alexandra walked quickly to be enfolded into Dmitri's arms.

"I'm so glad you're here! This is going to be hard," she said, swallowing a hard lump in her throat.

"I know, *Sashka*. I wouldn't make you face this alone."

She looked up into his eyes, finding them filled with compassion and tenderness. He bent his head down to touch his lips to hers. The zing of electricity shot through her body down to her toes, then raced back up to settle between her legs. She enjoyed the sensation, but realized it had to be ignored.

"Thanks."

He inclined his head to indicate the room they were about to enter.

"Many of the gang are already here. Emma was hoping to catch you before you walked in. Tom doesn't look like you remember him, so be strong."

She shot a quick look at him. "They never look like they did when alive."

He nodded. "True."

She entered the room and deliberately strode directly over

to the open casket. Since she was forewarned, she didn't gasp with surprise at how unlike the sandy-haired young man he looked. Tears sprang to her eyes as she remembered the many moments of pleasure they had shared. She reached forward to touch his hands and steeled herself for the coldness of the flesh. She stood still for a moment.

Dmitri stood silently and protectively behind her. She was grateful for his strength and solid presence, which her body seemed hyper aware of even though he made no sound.

Finally Alexandra took a deep breath and used both hands to unbutton the top few buttons of her blouse. She reached a hand down into her bra and pulled out a scarf that was a riot of colors: blues, teals, greens, all swirled around on a soft, opaque silk square. She held it up to her nose and breathed in, then she leaned over and trailed it across Tom's face. She ignored the gasps from behind Dmitri, and carefully folded the scarf into a tiny square, then placed it into the breast pocket of the last jacket Tom would ever wear.

"You always liked seeing me in that one, honey," she said softly as she patted the side of his face gently. "So take it with you. I made sure it smells like me and my perfume, since you liked that too. I'm gonna miss you, sweetie..."

Her shoulders suddenly shook as she was wracked with sobs. Dmitri moved up to hold her around the waist and he leaned his head forward to murmur into her ear as he guided her to the side where pictures were mounted on posters to illustrate Tom's happier moments. He kept his arm around her waist as he pointed to pictures as if she could actually see them through her tears, buying her time to get her emotions under control before she had to face anyone else.

Emma was suddenly at her other side and she rubbed Alexandra's arm and shoulder, providing a second barrier to prying eyes. They stood quietly for a while as the conversations picked back up again. Many of the people talked louder than usual so that she would hear the disapproval in their voices aimed at her for her behavior.

"Don't listen to them, honey," Emma said quietly. "You did what Tom would have appreciated the most. You honored the times you shared with him with a personal gesture that was sweet and touching. He'll be happy to take that scarf with him."

Alexandra blew her nose once again and smiled at Emma.

"I know. I just didn't expect it to hit me so hard. But I've never had to bury someone I had sex with before. Grandparents, yes. Older aunts and uncles, certainly. But someone who was younger than me? Someone who enjoyed life so much? It's so unfair."

"Yes it is," Dmitri agreed. "But take it from a Russian, life is unfair. It's filled with misery and pain, and the only escape is to die."

Alexandra turned to him with a quizzical look on her face.

"Really? That's how you really think?"

He shrugged. "It's how I was raised to think. On occasion I have been pleasantly surprised at how delightful life can be."

She punched his upper arm. "You'd better say something like that, mister!"

Emma pulled at her arm. "There's Tom's Mom. You should go talk to her and his brother before the family gloms onto them again to keep them away from us. They've been acting like we're crashing the wake…like we don't belong here."

Alexandra took a deep breath and straightened up, moving her shoulders back so that her considerable décolletage was even more pronounced.

"Then let's give them something to talk about after we're gone."

She put some extra swing into her hips as she strode over to pay her respects to Tom's immediate family.

"I'm so sorry, Mrs. Taylor," she said as she approached the sad-eyed older woman.

No one was more surprised than Alexandra when Tom's mother held out her arms and enfolded her in a hug.

"I know how much Tom enjoyed being with you and the other riders," she said loudly, as if ensuring the eavesdroppers would hear as well. "He used to talk about how happy he was when you would go on long trips together, or even just up to your family's place. He thought a lot of you, Alexandra. I'm glad he had such good friends in his life."

Alexandra felt the huge lump in her throat again, but spoke around it. "I'll never forget him, Mrs. Taylor. He had a way of smiling that made you really believe that wherever we were, was the best place to be. And when the sun played with his sandy hair, it looked like corn silk. He was great fun to be around. He'll be missed."

Tom's mother let her go and her eyes had the same unshed

tears that Alexandra's were holding. They nodded at each other and Alexandra turned to embrace Tom's brother as well. Their hug was quick and casual.

"You don't ride, do you?" she asked him. He shook his head.

"That's what Tom said. You never wanted to do the things he did because he was your older brother. But he was really proud of your grades in college. You keep on getting A's and graduate, and he'll be right next to you, cheering you on when you get your degree."

His eyebrows rose. "He talked about me to you guys?"

"Of course he did. He said we were like his second family, but he praised his hard-working Mom who had raised you both after your dad died and he was always bragging about how smart his baby brother was. He was so proud of you."

"Thanks," he said. He turned away from her suddenly. She gave him the split second of privacy he needed to pull himself together.

She felt her arm being touched by Dmitri and she reached down to hold his hand as they walked back to where the other bikers stood in a knot off to one side in the back of the room. She looked around, nodding to acknowledge everyone.

"You all heard about Jim, right?" she asked.

There were nods from everyone except Dmitri, who looked puzzled.

"Drive-by shooting Saturday while he was making a delivery in one of the crappy neighborhoods they sent him into," she explained. "That's why he's not here."

"Neither is Rich," Steve pointed out.

"He's not here yet?" Alexandra asked looking around. "He must have gotten stuck working late or in traffic."

"There he is," Bob inclined his head towards the main door. Rich walked in and made his way to the coffin. He kneeled in front of it, bowed his head and crossed himself. He got up and looked around and seeing them at the back, strode past all of the people he didn't know to get to them.

"Sorry I'm late," he said as he approached them. "Bad traffic."

"It's okay. I'm just glad you made it," Alexandra said. She turned to answer a question from Katie.

Dmitri wasn't sure but he swore he saw a look of disapproval on the newcomer's face as he noticed Dmitri still held Alexandra's hand. Dmitri stared at him and when Rich looked up, the antipathy in his eyes was obvious...but only until Alexandra turned back and it disappeared suddenly.

"Isn't that the detective investigating Tom's accident?" Alexandra asked as she looked over Rich's shoulder. "I wonder what he's doing here."

Dmitri let go of her hand. "I'm going downstairs to the bathroom, then maybe outside for a smoke."

"Okay," she said as Rich moved to stand closer to her now Dmitri had gone from her side.

"What's up with him? Spooked by the cop?" he asked conversationally.

Alexandra shrugged. "Who knows? Maybe he just has to pee."

The bikers continued to talk amongst themselves about the two recent losses their gang had experienced. After about a half-hour of chatting idly, they decided they had been there long enough to pay their respects to their comrade. They had already decided they would all ride their Harleys to the funeral in the morning, so they could make a fierce noise as they rode together in the procession.

They began to drift out in pairs, stopping to tell Tom's family good-bye before they left. Alexandra waited for Dmitri to come back, but eventually the only ones left were Rich and her.

"I think I'll go out and look for him," she announced to Rich.

"Maybe he's gone home already," he suggested.

"I don't think so. I'll see you tomorrow morning, okay?"

"Fine."

She turned and walked up to tell Tom's mother and brother their plans.

"We'll ride as a gang in the procession. But none of us will be staying for the luncheon. I'll have to get back to work. And besides, we don't want to intrude. The wake and funeral are more public. The luncheon is for family."

"If you reconsider, you are welcome to come," Tom's mother insisted as she hugged Alexandra.

"I'll keep that in mind. See you in the morning."

Alexandra decided to check the rooms downstairs to see if Dmitri was there. He wasn't in the room that held the industrial-sized coffee urn.

Might as well pee before I hit the road.

After she was done, she walked towards the stairs leading up to the chapel. Suddenly Detective Jones was at her side.

"Have you been waiting for me?" she demanded. "It's like you're spying on me or something. You don't suspect me of anything, do you?"

"No. But we had a tip today I thought you should know about."

She sighed. "Look, I'm really tired. I haven't had any dinner and I'll be working late tomorrow to make up for attending the funeral. Can't this wait?"

"It'll only take a few minutes. We had an anonymous call come in to the station after you left this afternoon. Some guy said he had seen someone push a dark car into a lake south by Hastings. We sent a guy out there and sure enough there was a car submerged there. No one would have seen it through the weeds, unless they knew to look for it. We had it pulled up and traced it to a rental car place here in St. Paul."

"Was it the car that hit Tom?"

"It might be. It had some damage that might indicate it was involved in an accident."

"Did you find out who rented it?"

"We talked to the owner of the place it was rented from. He said a guy rented it from him early on Friday morning. He said the guy insisted on paying cash and used the name Mike Smith on the information forms. He said he didn't have a license because he had lost it. When the owner balked, he offered to pay an extra c-note so he could still get the car."

"That all sounds really suspicious to me," she said. "And I'm not a cop. I've just seen things like that on TV and movies. Does he tape his customers?"

"No, that's just the problem. And the guy had on a leather jacket, a hat, dark sunglasses, and what looked like a fake beard. But there was one thing the rental guy remembered."

"What?"

"The guy had some kind of an accent. He thought it was Slavic...maybe Russian."

Alexandra felt all of the color drain out of her face.

"Is there something wrong, Miss Blackstone? Do you know someone with a Russian accent?"

"Yes," she answered in a whisper. "He..." She cleared her throat and began again, "He joined our gang about four months ago."

"What can you tell me about him?"

Besides the fact that I'm in love with him? Besides the fact that he's told me he won't be happy until he has me to himself? Besides the fact that he's jealous of all of the men in my gang?

She could feel herself hyper-ventilating while the detective stood and watched her intently. She forced herself to make words come out of her mouth.

"Um, his name is Dmitri."

"Dmitri what, Miss Blackstone? We need a bit more to go on than a first name."

Her mind had gone blank.

"I don't know his last name. Are you going to pick him up?"

"We'd like to talk to him…that's all. We need to ask him a few questions. Do you know where we can reach him?"

She shook her head. "No, I don't know where he lives. He used to work as a weeknight bouncer for one of the places we drink at on weekend nights, but he quit that job about two weeks ago."

"Do you have a phone number we can try?"

Numbly, she nodded and pulled her cell phone out of her pocket. She scrolled through the numbers and read them in a monotone to the detective as he scribbled them down on a crumpled note pad.

"Thanks, Miss Blackstone."

"Is that all?"

"Yes."

"Then good-night."

"I'll walk you upstairs. I need to talk to the family of Tom Taylor before I leave."

As they neared the door to the chapel, Alexandra said, "Bye, Detective Jones."

"Goodbye. We'll be in touch. And don't leave town."

Alexandra tried not to rush but could feel her heart pounding as she finally reached the door and pushed it open to feel the hot summer air on her face. She was sweating despite the air-conditioning, yet also shivering from the cold.

She looked around and saw that all the bikes were gone. She walked quickly over to her SUV and hit the clicker to open the door. As her hand touched the handle and pulled up, she sensed a presence behind her.

"Are you alright, Alexandra?"

She felt herself trembling.

"I'm fine, Dmitri. Where'd you go? Did you smoke a whole pack out here?"

"No. If you'll remember, I'm in the process of getting myself a legal identity. But I'm not sure if it would hold up to official scrutiny yet, so I couldn't take any chances. I didn't want to answer any questions that detective might have had."

No! No! No! Not you! No!

She felt rooted to the spot, yet her heart was racing in panic. She was trapped in a nightmare where she needed to move, yet was unable to do so.

"Are you alright, *Sashka*?" He had leaned closer to her and was inhaling the scent of her hair.

"I'm...uh...I'm really tired. I need to be up early tomorrow for the funeral, then I'll have to change and head to the office and work really late to make up for the missing time. I don't think you should come back with me tonight. And I think I'll be too wiped out tomorrow night too."

He reached a hand forward to caress her neck and with one finger under her chin, he raised her face up to look into her eyes. She tried very hard to project a neutral face, but knew from the look on his face she was failing entirely.

"Alright, my love. You're under a lot of stress right now. I'll see you on Wednesday night, then."

She breathed in a deep breath. "Yeah. I'll probably be feeling better by then. It's just that with Tom's death and all... and now Jim's too. I'm feeling really freaked out. I need some alone time to process everything that's been happening."

He leaned forward to brush his lips against hers.

"Until Wednesday, then."

He reached over and finished opening her door and shut it behind her when she was in the seat. She pulled her seatbelt on and forced herself to smile at him once she had rolled the window down.

"Good-night, Dmitri."

He nodded and stood back as she drove out of the parking lot. Her last view of him was seeing him watching her drive off in the rearview mirror as she pulled into the street.

She held herself together until she got her car parked and was up in her condo. Then her control broke and she cried, long and hard. She mourned her murdered friends who had been her lovers. That was bad enough.

But to think that Dmitri might be the one who killed them? What the fuck for? To get me to himself? He's been doing a good job of that already...no need to kill anyone.

Is he capable of murder? Of course he is! He as much as told me he has killed before. He might have done this. He knows how to take a life. But is it him? How can the hands that make me so crazy with lust, be the same hands that pulled a trigger and killed Jim? How can the man who has moved so far into my life and my heart, be the one who killed Tom, whose whole life was ahead of him?

Holy shit! And what am I going to do about it? Cover for him? Or turn him in? And if I turn him in and he finds out, will he kill me too?

I've never been in love before. No man has ever been able to crawl so far into my head that I'd even consider covering for him, or lying for him. What am I gonna do?

It was late when she finally crawled into bed, the help she sought from the Reverend Jack Daniels only partially quieting the voices yelling in her head. What little sleep she got was fitful and not at all relaxing. She woke up almost more tired than she was the day before. Now she felt a bone-weariness that threatened to make her unable to even get out of bed. But there was a funeral to go to and she owed it to Tom to lead the other bikers in honoring him by riding along with him to his final resting place.

Chapter Thirteen

Alexandra dressed as if it was a Friday night and she was heading to the bar. The fact that she was drinking lots of coffee since it was morning leant a sense of surrealism to everything. Not that she needed anything else to remind her of the nightmare her life had become.

She picked out the business suit she'd change into when she raced back after the funeral, when she exchanged her Harley for her SUV. While taking a final look at herself in the mirror she stuck out her tongue.

You look like shit, girl! Dark circles under your eyes...everyone's gonna see you're not getting any sleep. And your eyes look haunted. If that cop is there he's gonna know you're hiding something. I did give him Dmitri's phone number, but I'm betting he's smart enough not to answer a call from a number he doesn't recognize.

I'll bet the detective will be at the funeral, but Dmitri won't. So much for being my support in my time of need. Fuck it all...time to head out.

* * * *

As she strode into the funeral chapel for the service before the procession to the cemetery, Alexandra kept her head high and her shoulders thrown back, emphasizing the size of her breasts that were barely contained in the leather halter she wore under her leather vest. Her upper arm tattoos were on display, and that, combined with her monumental cleavage and skin-tight jeans, caused plenty of loud whisperings of disapproval from those already gathered in the room. She had expected it and ignored it.

She kept her sunglasses on to hide her eyes as she walked in, and looked around for the others she knew were there because she had counted the Harleys in the lot. She was the last one to get there, and they only had to wait a few minutes before the minister made his way to the front of the room to begin the prayers that would lead up to the sealing of the coffin.

As he spoke she looked around for Dmitri, but didn't see him anywhere. But as she had suspected, Detective Jones was there, studying the gathering with impassioned eyes, since after all, this was just another part of his job.

After the prayers were done, everyone was invited to walk by the casket one more time to say their final farewells to Tom. His mom and brother were the first ones to approach him, and they remained there, huddled close to each other, the younger man trying hard to be strong for his weeping mother. The extended family members and friends were next, lining up to say goodbye before they headed out to their cars to get ready for the procession.

Finally once everyone else had been up, Alexandra led her gang up to take their last leave of their companion. Alexandra was the first one to stand with tears in her eyes, as she leaned over and gently kissed Tom's lips one last time.

She stood to the side with his mother and brother as the rest of her gang took their leave.

Bob put a pack of Tom's favorite cigarettes into the casket with him. Steve put in a pint of Jack Daniels. Katie put in a nosegay of flowers.

Chuck added a pack of poker cards, "In case he gets bored."

Angela put in a photograph from her ultrasound, "Because he was so excited to see the baby."

Brad put in a paperback, "His favorite sci-fi author," he explained.

Leann put in a quart of Tom's favorite beer. The rest just stood in silence or gave the biker salute to their fellow rider one last time.

Alexandra gave Tom's mother one last hug and nodded at her gang, "It's time for us to saddle up, people. Let's show everyone how we honor one of our own."

They walked together out to their bikes and fired them up in rapid succession, the throaty roars bouncing off of the funeral home and surrounding buildings to create a satisfyingly loud echo of noise. As Alexandra looked around with pride at her friends, she saw Detective Jones standing and talking with one of the relatives. He seemed to feel her gaze and looked up to nod at her. She nodded back in acknowledgement, then they all stuck the orange funeral stickers on their windshields and got ready to follow the procession.

The ride was uneventful. As Alexandra had expected, the loud roar of the bikes drew everyone's attention, and many stood respectfully or removed their hats as the procession went by. She had tears still unshed in her eyes.

See, Tom? Everyone can see how important you were to us. You didn't deserve this, honey. I'll do everything in my power to help find who cut you down, and make sure he pays.

From the back of her mind, or maybe from her heart, a tiny voice whispered, *Even if it's Dmitri?* She nodded as she rode. *Yes.*

As they stood around at the hole in the ground that Tom was to be lowered into, Alexandra had the feeling she was being watched. She kept looking around and thought she caught a glimpse of Dmitri behind a large nearby family tomb. But when she moved to get a better look, he was gone. As she moved again, she noticed that Detective Jones was watching her intently, and looked briefly in the direction she was looking before meeting her eyes. She decided to pay more attention to the prayer the minister was intoning before the body would be lowered into the grave.

Once the family had their chance to toss a clump of dirt onto the coffin, they thanked everyone for their attendance and invited them to join in a luncheon at a local restaurant. The people began to disperse back to their vehicles. Alexandra wasn't in the mood for talking, and neither were any of the other bikers. They silently returned to their bikes and fired them up. Since they were all heading in different directions, they headed off independently, or in pairs. Rich was the last one left standing with Alexandra.

"Are you alright, Alex?" he asked gruffly. "I know this is hard on you. Is there anything I can do to help? Maybe come and spend the night with you at your condo?"

Alexandra shook her head. "No, Rich, but thanks for asking. I've got to go change and head to my office, and I'll be working really late tonight, to make up for leaving early yesterday, and being late today. I'll barely have the energy to make it home and will probably collapse as soon as I get there."

He nodded. "If you think of anything I can do to help you deal with all of this, just call me. Anytime."

Since his bike was next to hers, they were standing close

together, which was the only way they heard each other over the sound of Rich's Harley. Rich leaned over and kissed Alexandra, a light touch at first, then gaining in pressure until she looked up at him in surprise as she backed away. She pushed at his hand that reached around her waist for her butt.

"Hold on, cowboy! I'm still reeling from burying one of my boys, and there's another funeral we'll have to attend soon. I've never been so not-in-the-mood in my life. I'm sure I'll recover eventually. But for now? Hands off."

"Fine," he growled, then turned and hopped on his bike to ride off.

She watched him ride off for a second then got on her bike. Before she could turn the key, Detective Jones stood next to her.

"Miss Blackstone, a minute, please?"

"What is it, Detective?"

"We've been unable to contact the man you call Dmitri. But I asked some of your friends and they indicated that he knows where your condo is. In fact, though none of them have ever been to it, he's spent the night with you. Is this true?"

"Yeah. So what?"

"So I'd like you to take my card with my number at the station on it and keep it on your person at all times."

She looked at the card then at the detective.

"Why?"

"Because I want you to call me if you're contacted or confronted by the man we want to talk to."

"What if I'm not at home?"

He nodded. "Give me a location and I'll find you. I'll use the GPS in your cell phone if I have to."

"But it'll still take time for anyone to get to me, right?"

He looked pained. "Sometimes it takes longer than other times. Depends on time of day, traffic, how many officers are busy elsewhere. That kind of stuff. But I can assure you, someone will be alerted that you need assistance the minute you call my number, even if I'm not there."

She held out her hand and he handed it to her.

"What are you going to do to Dmitri?"

He looked surprised but his face quickly went back to neutral.

"We just want to talk to him. Ask him a few questions. That's all."

She put the card into her bra top before staring at him, letting him see she noticed his eyes had followed her movements.

"Do you really think he's involved with this?"

He shrugged while looking up at her eyes. "I don't know. But we won't find out until we can ask him some questions."

"Okay. Fine. If I see Dmitri, I'll call. Anything to help find out who's been hunting my boys."

He nodded. "Good. Thanks."

She turned the key and fired up her Harley, the noise temporarily deafening both of them. She had to yell for him to hear her.

"Let me know if you find out anything. Bye."

He moved back and she rode her bike out onto the street, to head home to change into her businesswoman persona for the day.

* * * *

As she had expected, she had a very long and tiring day at the office. After work she barely made it home before she collapsed in exhaustion, falling asleep as soon as her head hit the pillow.

When the alarm went off the next morning, she toyed with smashing it against the wall. Accepting the inevitable, she got up to begin another grueling day trying to catch up on her work. She was living on coffee and adrenaline, which was not a very productive combination, but she had too much work to do, not much time to do it, and very little desire to do it at all. She had missed a few vital meetings, so she had to read a lot of emails to catch up on current projects. She met with her sales and marketing managers to get back into the loop on what they were working on and had a few messages she had to send to clients who expected the personal touch from the owner of the company.

I'm glad I'm too busy to think about the hell my personal life has become, she mused during a visit to the bathroom. *I just hope I can get some sleep tonight. I'll have clients in for meetings for the next two days, and I can't keep looking like a zombie with bloodshot eyes and dark shadows on my face. No one cares that I've just lost two very close friends. All they care about is that their business is being taken care of. So my head's gotta stay in the game.*

It was almost eight when she finally left the office. Her secretary was long gone, as were most of her employees. She had chased the cleaning crew away and told them to come back to do her office later. She nodded at their supervisor as she entered the elevator, to indicate she was leaving. She barely noticed anything on the short drive back to her condo. All she could think about was taking a long soak in her Jacuzzi and crawling into her bed to seek some oblivion.

As she turned the key then opened the door she knew he was there. The unmistakable aroma of freshly-cooked dinner assailed her nostrils.

Shit! Shit! He's here! How am I gonna alert the detective?

Dmitri had obviously heard her closing the door. He strode quickly into the room to enfold her in a bear hug. She had to force herself not to burst into tears because all she really wanted to do was let him continue to hug her. She wanted to tell him all of her problems and hear him comfort her. But there was the whole trust issue...

"*Sashka*! You look so tired, my love. But I have an apology to make to you."

For what? Killing my friends?

She cleared her throat, swallowing around the hard lump that threatened to make her cry.

"Um, I've gotta pee. There was a lot of traffic on the way here, and they had closed the bathroom on my floor for cleaning. Hold that thought and I'll be right back."

He nodded. "Of course. I'll pour you something to drink."

She quickly walked down the hall to the bathroom and turned on the exhaust fan. She dialed the number on the card she still had tucked into her bra. It rang five times before it was picked up by the detective himself.

"Hello?"

She tried a loud whisper. "Detective Jones? This is Alexandra Blackstone."

"Is this Miss Blackstone? I'm having trouble hearing you. Can you speak up?"

"Not really. I'm in my bathroom. He's here. Dmitri's in my condo."

"I'll grab a few officers and be there as soon as I can, Miss Blackstone. Keep him talking, but don't arouse his suspicions."

"Okay. Bye."

She put her phone back into her bra but put the detective's

business card under some towels in the linen cabinet. She flushed the toilet and made a face at herself in the mirror as she ran the water to simulate washing her hands.

Keep him talking, huh? How? Ask him who he's going to target next?

She was dismayed to notice her hands were shaking and her breathing rate had sped up.

Get control of yourself, Alex. You can't let him see you're scared of him. I am scared of him, right? Or is it just that I want him so badly I have to force my hands to not touch him? Shit...shit...shit!

She walked back down the hall and into the kitchen. Dmitri put some food onto a plate and placed it on the one side of the small table. She sat down heavily in the chair and took a sip of the beer he had poured into a glass for her.

"Goulash is the ultimate Russian version of stew," he explained as the delicious smells almost made her hungry enough to eat. As it was, the lump in her throat combined with the tears brimming just behind her eyes, and she was unable to swallow anything more substantial than the beer.

"Smells delicious, but I don't think I can eat anything." She took another sip from the glass.

He sat across from her, sipping his vodka on ice, studying her closely.

"You look like you haven't been eating or sleeping, *Sashka*. You need to do both to keep up your strength. Maybe you need a soak in the Jacuzzi and a back rub, to relax you enough for you to get some rest."

She swirled the beer around before she asked, casually she hoped, "What is it you wanted to apologize to me for?"

His lips twitched in amusement at her question.

"I didn't realize just how late you were going to stay at the office. I got hungry, once the goulash was done, and even though I meant to wait for you, I couldn't help myself. So I've already eaten. I'm sorry...I know that's rude. But I don't mind watching you eat. I'll enjoy seeing you enjoy my cooking."

That's it? That's all you're sorry for?

She shook her head. "I don't think I can eat. I'm too stressed. Tom's funeral was today. You weren't there to support me, were you?"

He looked solemn. "I didn't think it was wise to be seen in public where the policeman would have a chance to question me."

"Why not? What're you afraid of?" She tried not to sound accusing, but from the surprised look on his face, she failed.

"I told you, Alexandra, I'm in the process of getting a legal identity. But these things are not as easy as they used to be, back before everything was so computerized. Hacking into federal records is chancy no matter which system you're breaking into. The agent who is doing this for me is taking a huge risk by doing it."

"Then why's he helping you?"

"Because I'm calling in a marker, and *she* wants things cleared between us."

Despite everything, Alexandra felt an instantaneous spark of jealousy.

"She? No wonder you stayed so long out of town."

His lips curved upwards for an instant as he stared at her face. "There's no need for you to be jealous of any woman, *Sashka*...ever. I stayed because she needed my help in creating me an identity. She has the right to expect I won't get picked up, which would require a background check when it's not ready for that kind of scrutiny yet. That would not only result in my being deported, it would expose her to repercussions from her illegal actions. I'm protecting her as much as myself, by avoiding answering any official questions at this point in time."

"So that's why you ducked out of the wake when the detective walked in?"

"Yes."

"Not because you're afraid of what he would ask you?"

He leaned back in his chair and watched her closely. He spoke softly, with sadness in his voice.

"Is that what you really think? Is that the opinion you have of me, after all we've shared?"

Alexandra felt a tear roll down her cheek and she ignored it. She felt herself getting angry, which at least was familiar enough to allow her more control than the overwhelming sadness she was afraid to wallow in.

"Why wouldn't I? You're a killer. You told me that the first time I met you. You know how to kill and you've done it before. Why not now? You've told me that you want me for yourself. Seems like eliminating the competition would be the best way to do that."

She watched as his hands shook while he lifted the glass to

his lips to take another sip of his vodka. When he spoke again his words sounded heavy, as if it hurt him to say them.

"Alexandra, I don't know how to say this so you will believe me. But I had nothing to do with the deaths of your two friends."

"Just a coincidence that you were out of town for both of their murders, then, huh?"

"Yes."

"Someone's trying to set you up, right?"

"Yes."

She spoke without even thinking of the repercussions of tipping him off to what she knew. She lashed out at him with pent-up frustration and anger.

"So someone else rented the car that was used to hit Tom, then turned around the next day and drove by Jim to shoot him? Someone else dumped the car into a nearby lake? Someone else rented the car paying cash because he had no license...but he *did* have a Russian accent?"

He stood up and walked over to the counter to pour himself more vodka, his back to her. His next words astounded her.

"Wot, me luv? 'E 'ad an occent? Not lak a Cockney?"

"Perhaps he sounded more like a British gentleman, who was schooled at Eton and Cambridge?" Now he sounded like James Bond.

"Or mie-be he sawnded lak a southenuh, from Geor-giah? And ah mean the one near Waw-shing-tun, Day-Say, nat the wun in Russ-ky-la-yand."

He turned to look into her eyes.

"Name an English-speaking area of the world, Alexandra. I can probably do the accent well enough to pass, at least to a non-native. And I can do accents in many other languages as well."

She sputtered, "But you always talk with a Slavic accent..."

"Yes, when I'm being myself. When I'm relaxed. It's how I originally learned to speak English. But it's not the only accent I know. If I was trying to cover my tracks, wouldn't I have used any of a dozen other accents, rather than the one that would lead everyone directly to me?"

Her anger was leaving her and she felt even more vulnerable.

"But you've been telling me since you met me that you want

me for yourself. You walked out on me at the barn because of that. You're the only one who has ever said that to me..."

He walked back to sit down heavily on the chair, as if weighed down by the importance of what he was saying.

"My sweet, impetuous, wonderful Alexandra. You're so much like a man in so many ways, holding your own in business situations and riding herd over a bunch of unruly bikers in your off-time. But you really don't understand the mind of a man, do you?"

"What do you mean?"

"I'm not the only man who wants you to myself, Alexandra," he said softly. "I'm just the only one to be honest enough to tell you that."

"But no other guy in the gang ever said that."

"No, but many thought it. When a man has great sex with a woman, we are hard-wired to want that woman to ourselves. They only shared because you made it clear it was either that or lose the chance to have sex with you again. The jealousy directed at me when I was in the bar with you came from many of the men in your gang. I was even told that sooner or later I'd have to get used to being just one of your men. I said I'd leave before it came to that. And I meant it."

"Then why are you still here?"

He leaned forward. "Because I thought I was making progress with you. I originally only intended to stick around long enough to see if I could tame the fiery, redheaded, wildcat biker queen. I didn't expect you to be everything I have ever wanted in a woman. I didn't expect you to be my equal in every important way, including but not limited to, in bed. And I certainly didn't expect to fall in love with you. But I did."

Alexandra felt the lump in her throat threatening to render her speechless, and the tears flowed freely down her face.

"You did?"

"Yes."

He reached across the table to hold the hand that wasn't wrapped around the beer glass.

"Honey, at least one other man wants you for himself. That's the man who was directing the most amount of jealousy towards me. That's the one who has decided that I'm the competition that must be eliminated. And what better way to do it than to use what you already told them about me, that as part of my former life I have committed murder in the past, and leave clues that point directly to me as being the killer. This way two other men are gone, and I'll be sent to jail or deported. Either way, that will leave you defenseless and mostly alone. And that man will step in to comfort you in your loss."

"But who would do that?"

"I don't know. But I swear to you by all that's holy, and by the graves of my grandparents, that it wasn't me, Alexandra. I love you, but I won't kill to keep you. I'd kill to keep you safe, but that's different."

He took a deep breath and looked into her eyes. She was astounded by the pain she saw there.

"Murder is a hard thing to do. I've done it when ordered to, and I've done it when it was him or me. But it's not to be done lightly or easily. Years ago I made the split-second choice not to kill the woman who is creating my legal identity. She knew it and said she owed me. That's why she's taking such a risk for me.

But if it came to you deciding that having other men is more important than being with me, I'd leave town. There would be no further reason for me to stay. And I'd go back to the constant motion of a man with no allegiance to anyone or anything. I've lived like that for a very long time. It's just that… I thought I had finally found a reason to belong somewhere."

She was sobbing now, her words mostly garbled.

"But you know so many ways to kill, you said…"

"Since I *do* know so many ways to literally get away with murder, why on earth would I be so sloppy as to leave so many clues pointing directly to me?"

She jumped at a sudden noise from the hall outside of her condo and stood up quickly, remembering.

"You have to go! Dmitri, you have to get out of here!" Alarm was in her voice.

He stood and took the few steps to enfold her in his arms.

"Why? Are you still afraid of me?"

"No! I called the police when I got home! They're probably almost here! You've got to get out of here before they get here! Oh, Dmitri, I'm so sorry! I didn't know what to think or believe! I thought it was you and it was tearing me apart!"

He caressed the side of her face with one hand and turned her head up to look into her eyes.

"And now?"

"You need to get out of here! Please! I'm sorry I called! I'm sorry I didn't trust you! Just go!"

He lowered his head and crushed her lips with his, as he pulled her so close she could feel his heartbeat. She moaned and twined her arms around him, capitulation in every part of her body that molded itself to him.

There was a loud knock on the door.

"It's them! Go!"

He nodded. "I'll contact you soon. I'll think of a plan to catch the real murderer. "

"How are you going to get out?"

"You're only on the twelfth floor. And there are balconies outside. Remind me to tell you someday about the time I escaped from a penthouse on top of a skyscraper with no balconies. This is a piece of cake."

The knocking got louder and more insistent.

She pushed him away from her, desperation in her voice. "Go…now!"

He strode over to the balcony in the living room and slid the door open. He turned to blow her a kiss.

"I love you, Dmitri!"

The happy smile he gave her lit her soul with joy.

"Then I promise you, nothing can hurt us or keep us apart."

He swung a leg over the balcony, then he was gone. She turned to walk over to the front door that was being pounded on continuously.

She took a deep breath before she unlocked the door. It was pushed open quickly and her living room was suddenly full of uniforms and one very irate-looking detective.

"Where is he?" He demanded.

Alexandra took a deep breath. "He's gone. He left about fifteen minutes ago."

He stared into her face, trying to decide if he believed her or not. She kept her face as neutral as she could, while trying not to look as guilty as she felt.

"I told you to keep him here."

"I tried to. But he said he had an appointment and he was just here to make me dinner. Then he left."

The other officers returned from searching the other rooms. They shook their heads at his questioning look.

"He's not here, sir," said the one who had come from the bedroom.

"There's food in the kitchen, and signs that someone ate already, and a plateful is set for another person. But he's gone."

Detective Jones looked around the room.

"The balcony door is open. Check the balcony...maybe he's out there."

Alexandra was practicing deep-breathing to calm herself down as the officer went onto the balcony, looked around and directly down. He re-entered the living room shaking his head.

"No sign of him, sir."

Detective Jones turned to Alexandra with an accusing stare.

"You aren't covering for him in any way, are you, Miss Blackstone?"

She reached inside of herself for the anger she felt at the perpetrator.

"Why would I? I want the guilty person caught and punished! Tom and Jim were my friends. Very close friends. I want their deaths avenged in the most painful way possible. So, no. If I had any suspicion he was the one responsible for the funerals I've been dreading, I'd never cover for him."

"You didn't by any chance share anything I told you with him, did you?"

"Why would I do that?"

He stared at her for a long moment.

"Why, indeed." He looked around at the uniformed officers. "Alright, guys. I think we're done here."

He turned back to Alexandra. "This time I was too late. But I want you to call me the next time he contacts you in any way. Is that clear?"

Alexandra nodded.

"And don't..."

"Don't leave town...yeah, I know. You've said that before," she interrupted him.

He turned and followed the uniformed officers out the door.

Alexandra let out a huge sigh of relief once she was able to lock the door behind them. She went out onto the balcony herself and looked around, gazing at the drop down to the ground from up there.

"So this is a piece of cake for you, huh? Dmitri, I have the feeling you could share stories with me for the rest of our lives, and still I wouldn't hear all of them."

She went back in and looked at the food he had put on the plate for her.

I'll bet I could eat some of that. I am kind of hungry, now that I think about it. Maybe I'll just warm it up a little.

As the plate spun in the microwave, she got another beer out of the fridge and twisted the cover off. When the food was done she sat and put a forkful into her mouth and chewed experimentally.

Wow! Yum! Just like everything else you've cooked for me. I really don't deserve you, Dmitri. But once this is all over, assuming we both survive, I'm going to spend a really long time trying to make you believe I deserve you...even if I don't.

After eating, Alexandra made her way to the Jacuzzi and soaked while she finished her beer. Then she crawled into her bed and settled down, hugging the pillow Dmitri's head had rested on the last night he was with her. She sniffed it deeply. Satisfied it smelled like him, she smiled.

The next thing she knew, her alarm was going off and it was morning and time to get ready for work. She stretched and rolled over, feeling more rested than she had for days.

Not out of the water yet, but I trust Dmitri will be able to figure this whole thing out. He's good at so many things. I just have to trust him. And I do...I really, really do.

Chapter Fourteen

Alexandra was so busy at work on Thursday she didn't have any time to worry about Dmitri. While she was on her lunch break, sitting at her desk eating some soup, she got a call from Angela letting her know the wake and funeral for Jim had been postponed to the following Monday because they were waiting for all of his out-of-town relatives to arrive.

"So Monday night will be the wake and Tuesday will be the funeral."

Alexandra sighed heavily. "Just like this week, huh? What a shitty way to start a week."

"Yeah, but at least you're the boss at your job. When I told my boss I'd need off on Tuesday morning again, you'd have thought I was asking for a month off, judging by the bitching he did. I mean, I never take any time off all year, and he begrudges me two late starts due to funerals for two of my closest friends? What a dickhead!"

"You want I should make an appearance there right after the funeral, before I get a chance to change into my business-persona? I can scare the shit out of him and still be here before lunchtime."

Angela giggled. "I'll bet you could. No, not this time. But if he tries to give me any crap when I'm taking time off for my wedding, or to have my baby, I'll take you up on that offer."

"You got it. It will be part of my wedding present to you."

"Um, have you heard from Dmitri? The cops have been asking a lot of questions about how much we know about him."

"No. I don't know where he is, but I know in my heart he's not the one who's been hunting my gang. Someone else is, and there's gotta be some way to find out who."

"I wish I could help. But I'm getting the evil eye from my boss now. Jesus, I'm sitting at my desk snarfing my food here, so I'm not even wasting *his* time making any calls. I've gotta go. Talk to you later, okay? Maybe see you tomorrow night?"

"We'll see. Depends on how I feel after a grueling day

spent meeting with demanding clients all day. But maybe, okay? Bye."

"Goodbye, Alex."

Alexandra leaned back in her chair and stared out the window for a while.

Should I go tomorrow night? I know Dmitri won't come, in case Detective Jones has someone watching the place. None of the cops know what he looks like, but if he's right and it's someone in my gang, then that guy is bound to alert the police if he shows up.

And who can it be? Not Bob, certainly, since he and Emma are getting married so he doesn't even want me anymore. Ditto José, since he and Angela have a baby on the way. That leaves Steve, and he's not that hot-blooded of a guy. I never got the feeling he cared whose hole he was poking, as long as he got laid. Chuck? I kind of thought he was getting sweet on Katie, but she seems to be oblivious. And Brad? I know Valerie had a real heavy-duty crush on him when he joined us last year. And every time we've had play-time, she's been sucking him off at some point.

That leaves Rich, and he's the only one I'm really worried about. He's got a real temper. Plus he's the only one who has ever really wanted to play rough. No one else raises welts on the gals with the riding crop...but he does. He's the one who enjoys scaring people when we're in new bars. He also tends to hurt people when we're having a rumble with another gang. Mike wouldn't let him go with him to New Orleans when he moved last year because he said Rich picks too many fights. And Craig almost threw us out of the bar he co-owns with that babe he met in Sturgis, when we were out there last summer and Rich broke her brother's nose.

Her alarm went off to remind her she needed to get herself back to thinking about her business, because she had a client due to arrive in less than a half-hour and she needed to review his file.

This has to wait until later.

* * * *

Once again it was after eight when Alexandra finally got home. This time there were no enticing aromas to greet her when she walked in, but she was too bone-tired to care. Her brain hurt from mental sparring with clients all day, and her body ached from stress. The first thing she did was tear off her business clothes and change into shorts and a T-shirt. Then she hit the treadmill and ran a quick six miles, mostly uphill. She lifted weights for another twenty minutes, then followed up with sit-ups and push-ups until every muscle in her body ached from over-use, not stress.

She got the water running to fill the Jacuzzi while she cut up cheese and fruit, then brought that, along with a bottle of a nice Cava into the bathroom with her. The Spanish sparkling wine was dry enough to enhance the cheese and the fruit. She picked at the food while she soaked. Once she was beginning to feel pruned, she got up and carried her impromptu dinner into her bedroom. She continued to nosh while she looked through her personal emails and checked the news of the day for anything to keep her mind off of her own problems.

She was reading the obituary for Jim when her phone buzzed with a text. She picked it up quickly and saw it was from Dmitri. Wondering why he didn't call her, since she missed his voice along with his presence, she called up the text and read it.

Your phone may be tapped. Go to bar tomorrow. Tell everyone you want to be alone at farm next day...to mourn in peace.

Okay, she thought. *I guess I'm the bait to get the murderer to follow me out there, thinking he'll get me to himself.*

Her phone buzzed again.

Tell detective to hide with back-up in barn. Get who-ever shows up to go into the barn with you then you go into house. I'll ride up and confront him in barn.

Be careful! She texted back.

She leaned back on her pillow and drank the last of the sparkling Cava as she thought about Dmitri's plan.

This could work. Or it could go very wrong. I'll need to go see the Detective during my lunch break tomorrow. Not much time to convince him. Since he's supposed to be hiding, what if he doesn't show up? What if Dmitri gets a confession and there's no one there to hear it? No way around it. I'll have to go back into the barn after I hear Dmitri go in there.

I'm not an agent like you, Dmitri. But I'd do anything to help you prove your innocence. So, I'll just have to pretend to be the bad-ass everyone thinks I am, and hope we all survive to laugh about it later.

She reached over and turned out the lights, but sleep proved to be elusive for a long time. She ended up having to pleasure herself with her trusty weeknight lover, the battery-operated Mister Big, while imagining it was Dmitri who slid in and out of her. Eventually she fell into a fitful sleep.

* * * *

Alexandra had yet another late night at work, though not quite as late as the previous night's simply because she made herself leave before seven. She was too nervous about the part she had to play in trying to force the killer to out himself. Once she had changed into her biker queen regalia, she stared gravely at herself in the mirror.

Black leather halter showing maximum cleavage? Check. Skin-tight jeans shorts that show my ass cheeks when I bend over to make a shot at the pool table? Check. Tattoos all showing to let everyone know what a bad-ass I am? Check. Dark red and black striped nail polish on my fingers and toes? Check. High-heeled sandals so I'm taller than some men, and so my ass is nice and tight while I swing my hips when I walk? Check.

She leaned closer to peer at her face in the mirror.

Enough makeup so the circles under my eyes aren't so dark and noticeable? Check. Blush to be sure I have color, though I'm not eating, sleeping, or even feeling like normal? Check.

She stuck out her tongue at her image and grimaced.

Then I'm ready to do this. If it will help find and trap the killer, and allow for Dmitri to come back to me, then I'm more than ready. I just hope his identity is iron-clad enough by now so that when Detective Jones starts asking him questions, he will show up as legally allowed to be here. That, more than anything else, will let me know he's been telling me the truth.

She strode decisively over to the door and with a last look around her condo, she pulled the door closed, locked it, and headed down to the garage for her Harley.

* * * *

Alexandra laughed as she finished chugging the second

beer faster than she had chugged the first one. Cheers rang out from all around her as her gang celebrated that she was still the queen of chugs.

"Hey, did you think I forgot how?" She yelled at her gang. "I've been in mourning, but I'm still here. And I'm still thirsty! Pour me another one, Brad!"

"So, what kind of beer's in the keg you're getting delivered tomorrow?" Brad was busy pouring more beer into her glass from the over-sized pitcher.

"Ah, that's what I wanted to tell you all," she began, looking all around so everyone would gather to listen.

"Are we gonna have a ceremony to honor Tom and Jim?" asked Steve.

Alexandra shook her head. "Not tomorrow. I was figuring to wait until after Jim's wake and funeral. So next weekend we'll have a huge-ass bonfire in their honor. I think everyone should find something that makes you think of them, and you can throw that in so it follows them."

"So, no partying this weekend at your place?" Rich asked.

"No. I'm not in a partying kind of mood. In fact, I'm going to head out there by myself tomorrow. I want to be alone for a while. I need some solitude to think things through."

"What kind of things?" Rich asked, studying her face.

Alexandra shrugged. "I don't know. Just things."

"You're not gonna break up the gang, are you?" Katie leaned forward, both elbows on the table, giving everyone a great view of her cleavage. Chuck's eyes grew big as he sucked in a breath so audible Alexandra laughed.

"Dude! Ask her on a fucking date already! You don't have to wait until we're at my place to pair up, you know. Just ask Bob and Emma, or José and Angela! Right, people?"

There was a ripple of laughter around the table as those named called out their agreement, and Chuck blushed slightly while Katie's eyes narrowed speculatively as she studied his reaction.

Alexandra leaned back in her chair, balancing on the back two legs like her mother had always told her not to. She rocked slightly as she spoke.

"No, I have no plans to break up the gang. But things are changing around us and we have to decide how we're gonna react to those changes. I had hoped I'd have me a biker king at my side, but he seems to have disappeared."

"Maybe he's just out of town again?" Leann suggested.

"Or maybe he's on the run from the cops," Rich growled.

Everyone turned to look at him in surprise, so Alexandra asked, "What makes you think that?"

"He ran outta Tom's wake like his ass was on fire when the detective showed up. He didn't come to the funeral and no one has seen him since before two guys in our gang were killed."

"Correction, dude. I saw him last Saturday night, when he got back to town."

"Kind of suspicious, that he was out of town until after Jim was shot, huh?"

Alexandra tried to keep her face and tone neutral. "You think so?"

Brad spoke up. "He might be avoiding us because he thinks we suspect him."

"Or he's just avoiding the cops, since he's not here legally," suggested Valerie.

Alexandra shrugged. "Who knows? Anyway, I'm going out there alone tomorrow and I don't want any company. Got that everyone?"

She looked around to a general chorus of *yes* and heads nodding.

"We'll have our celebration of the passing of two of our members next Saturday. And that will be a party to remember. Got it?"

"To the party!" yelled Bob, holding his glass up in a toast.

Everyone held up their glass and echoed his words, and Alexandra felt a lump in her throat again.

Shit! I can't start crying again! What the fuck is wrong with me? I used to be able to handle anything without blinking an eye. But now? I can't seem to stop feeling raw and fragile, like my emotions are way too close to the surface.

Rich tapped her on the shoulder.

"Hear what's playing? It's your song, Queen."

Alexandra stared at him as she heard the chorus of the song about the woman who could rock your world all night long.

"So?"

"You wanna dance?"

"I'm not really in a dancing kind of mood. In fact, I need to pee. I'm gonna hit the can. Maybe someone else will dance with you..."

She ignored the irritated look on his face and slid off her barstool. She made sure to swing her hips on the way through the crowd and was rewarded by open-mouthed stares and grunted appreciation.

She pushed the door open and went into the lounge area of the small bathroom. Even though she'd been unaware she'd been followed, Emma walked through the door right after her.

"You okay, Alex?"

"Yeah, I just gotta pee." Alexandra pushed into the stall and did her business while Emma continued to talk to her.

"You really gonna go out there alone tomorrow? Doesn't sound like a smart idea to me, what with the person who's been hunting our gang still not caught."

"Too fucking bad. When have you ever known me to be afraid of anything or anyone?"

"Is Dmitri meeting you out there? Is that why you don't want anyone else to come?"

There was a loud flushing sound then Alexandra opened the door to meet the worried look on her friend's face with a shake of her head and a smile.

"No, Emma. I really do think being up there alone will be good for my head. I'm distracted at work, and not able to concentrate on much of anything. I can't let my personal business interfere with running the company. So I'm hoping having time to myself will do the trick. Or at least get me ready for another grueling week that's gonna start with a wake and funeral again."

Emma reached out and Alexandra allowed the hug to happen. She wasn't usually very comfortable with expressions of emotions, but Emma was her closest female friend. Emma seemed to take more comfort in it than Alexandra did, but as she pulled back, Emma smiled broadly at her.

"I hope you find what you're looking for out there tomorrow," Emma said. "You know, now I think about it, I've gotta pee too." She pushed open the stall door and went inside.

Alexandra washed her hands and checked her appearance in the dingy mirror above the sink. With a final grimace at herself, she opened the door and called out, "See you back at the bar, okay?"

"Be right out," Emma responded.

The rest of the evening played out as it usually did, with multiple pitchers of beer being consumed, along with some pizzas they had delivered to the bar.

I really miss having Dmitri around to drive me home, Alexandra thought as she stood up to walk to the bathroom again. *I've been getting used to having him as my designated driver so I could drink as much as I want. But I should be leaving soon anyway. I don't wanna be hung-over tomorrow morning when I'm gonna ride solo up to my place.*

When the lights blinked and the bartender announced it was time for the last call for alcohol, Alexandra surprised everyone including herself when she slammed her beer glass to the table and got up.

"That's it for me tonight, folks. I've gotta try to actually get some sleep before I ride solo tomorrow."

There were good-natured jibes accusing her of wimping out and being a lightweight, but she stared them all down.

Angela grinned at her.

"That's right, Queen. I'm the official lightweight around here now! I can't have any drinks until the baby's born. So no matter when you stop, you're still drinking more than me!"

Alexandra made a face at her. "Honey, I've *always* been able to drink more than you!"

There was general laughter as Angela grinned, nodding to acknowledge the truth. Alexandra made her way to the door then pushed it open to stride into the humid heat of the outside air. She fired up her bike then straddled it.

I've never walked out while there was still drinking to be done. Dmitri, this more than anything, proves how I feel about you!

Smiling at her own wit, she revved the engine and shot out into the street, unaware she was being watched by two sets of eyes. One was watching her for her protection. The other was watching with a sense of anticipation.

Chapter Fifteen

Ah, nothing better, Alexandra thought as she roared down the road, her red hair streaming behind her, the wind whistling in her ears. Once she had left the highway, the two-lane road was almost empty. So she thoroughly enjoyed herself, cruising along at any speed that felt right.

Why can't more of life be like riding? As long as you pay attention, nothing can hurt you. You control your destiny. A woman can be as good as a man, and when we pass each other, the biker salute lets us know we're not alone.

She enjoyed the ride so much she was surprised when she got to the turn-off that would take her to her family's place.

Actually, since Dad had me sign those papers last year and I took over paying the taxes, I have to stop thinking of this as Gram and Grampa's place. It's mine now. And good thing too! I can't even imagine the look on Dad's face if he ever saw what's in the barn! Yup, the pleasure area would blow him away!

She looked around carefully as she pulled onto the property. She had given the detective the code for the lock on the barn door. She hoped he was hiding in there…possibly with another cop or two, so that if the murderer did show up and confess, there would be enough muscle there to keep him from becoming violent. But since she had no idea if she was being watched, she resisted the urge to go into the barn and try to get anyone to respond.

There were no outward signs anyone was there. She had suggested a few places on the property where they could hide a car, but obviously there was no way to tell if they had taken her advice. She parked her Harley in its usual spot, right by the front porch and walked up to unlock the front door.

'Honey? I'm home!" She grinned as she called into the empty house and walked in. She stuffed her keys into the front pocket of her jeans, which was no easy feat considering how tight they were. Her phone was in the back pocket, so she figured she was ready for any emergency. She tossed the backpack that held her wallet along with some bottled waters and fruit, along with granola bars, onto the counter in the kitchen.

She checked the fridge and smiled. "Yup, there's beer here. Of course there is! I never let it get empty and we're sure to refill it before we leave, so there's cold ones waiting for us when we get here."

She opened the freezer. "And here's Dmitri's vodka. I don't know how he drinks that shit like it's water. It must be because he's Russian."

She tossed the bottles of water into the fridge and opened one, taking a long swallow. "Ah, that chases the road-dirt out of my throat. Listen to me! I'm talking to myself! Must be because I'm never alone out here."

She looked around trying to decide what to do. Her glance fell on a crossword puzzle book that Jim had left there on his last visit. She walked over and picked it up, then grabbed a pen off of the counter and headed out to the front porch.

She sat on one of the comfy couches on the front porch and began to work on the puzzle. *Jim wouldn't mind me working on his puzzles, right? And I'll burn this in the fire next weekend, so it follows you, okay, dude?*

It's really nice and peaceful out here. I should come out here alone more often. Maybe I really do need time to myself to recharge my batteries...or at least clear my head. That sun is really warm. I feel really relaxed...

Alexandra wasn't aware she'd drifted off until she was awoken by the loud roar of a Harley coming up the drive. She watched through her mirrored sunglasses as he rode up and parked next to her bike. Then he got up and strode up the stairs to lean against the railing in front of her.

"Rich! I told you I wanted to be alone up here." She tried to channel anger and not to let any fear or anxiety be reflected in her voice, but had no idea if she was succeeding or not.

He lit a cigarette and took a deep drag before he spoke. "Yeah, I know that's what you said. But what I *heard* was that you wanted me to come up to be with you, just the two of us. That's what you meant by alone, right?"

"What makes you think that?"

He stared at her intently, making her feel naked.

"You said you were hoping to have a king to ride by your side and rule the gang with you. Now Dmitri is out of the picture, I figured I'm the best candidate. So I'm here to audition for the part. I figure we can have a whole lotta fun out in the barn by ourselves. All those toys to play with, and no one waiting around for their turn. Just you and me and all of my nasty ideas of what I want to do to you."

Alexandra kept her eyes on his face, but was grateful she still wore her sunglasses, hoping they would hide how creeped out she was by his words.

"So, I'm gonna grab myself a beer from the kitchen. In fact I think I'll grab a few. Once we get busy, I'm not gonna want to stop for a beer run…even just into the house."

Shit! What do I do now? I'm supposed to let him into the barn then make an excuse to come back into the house. I sure hope this plan is going to go down like it's supposed to. I'm not looking forward to being the sole recipient of all of the violence Rich likes with his sex.

She forced herself to smile when Rich walked back onto the porch carrying a six-pack of beer.

"You think that'll be enough?" She tried for a light-hearted joke.

Rich nodded gravely. "To start with, but it's gonna be a long day."

She led the way as they walked across the yard to the barn. Alexandra could feel his eyes burning into her butt as every step brought them closer to him presumably getting what he wanted from her—capitulation.

Why didn't I notice this about him before? Shit, shit, shit! Poor Tom and Jim would still be here if I'd have thrown him out of the gang for excessive violence. I'm sorry, guys. It's all my fault.

She stopped at the barn and punched in the numbers to unlock the door. She could feel his body heat as he pressed himself closer to her back.

"Uh, there's a slight problem, dude."

"Problem?" His eyes narrowed as she turned around to face him and saw raw lust on his face.

"Uh, yeah. I wasn't expecting any company so I stopped for a burrito at El Grande on the way up here. You know what that shit always does to me."

He grunted. "I'll deal with it. I may have to punish you if it smells too bad." He leered.

Alexandra shook her head, "No. I mean I gotta go to the bathroom now. The sooner the better."

He took a step to the side and nodded at the house. "Then go. Get it out of your system now. I'll go in and get out some of the stuff I wanna use to play with you. That way I'll be ready and waiting for you when you get back."

"Fine. I'll be back in a few..."

She strode rapidly up to the front porch and went into the house. Once the door was closed she leaned against it weakly, trying not to hyperventilate.

Shit! Shit! Shit! It's really him! It's Rich! And he thinks that now he's eliminated the competition, he's got me where he wants me! Fucking A! What am I gonna do? If I spend too much time in the can he'll come up and drag me out! And if it doesn't stink in there he'll know I'm lying!

Taking a deep breath she walked up the stairs to the bathroom next to her bedroom.

It's got a better lock. Not that he's gonna let any lock keep him out.

She locked the door carefully then sat on the toilet seat and tried to take deep breaths. She looked at her watch. *I wonder how long I can get away with staying up here before he comes looking for me?*

Those ten minutes of watching time pass took forever. Alexandra was dripping with sweat and trying to control her racing heartbeat. She felt so nauseated she was toying with sticking her finger down her throat to make herself puke.

Suddenly the peace and quiet was shattered by the rumbling of another Harley roaring up the driveway. She looked out of the window and saw Dmitri pull up and park next to the other two bikes. He looked around before beginning to walk towards the barn.

Shit! If I tap on the window and he looks up, Rich might see if he's watching from the barn. That'll tip him off it's a set-up. So I can't call out to Dmitri either. I just hope his training as a spy included dealing with violent psychos.

She watched as Dmitri slowed down as he got closer to the door. He stopped and appeared to be listening, with his hand on the doorknob. He straightened and stood taller, as if he was getting himself ready for battle. He turned the handle and pushed the door open and went into the barn. The door closed behind him.

I know he told me to stay out of the barn, but I've got to know what's going on in there!

Alexandra rinsed her face with cold water and unlocked the door to follow Dmitri into the barn.

* * * *

All of Dmitri's senses were on alert as he walked through the door.

This guy's an amateur, but he's big and nasty, he thought as he carefully stepped into the dimly-lit barn.

Rich stood by a bale of hay cracking a whip. He wore only his jeans and a leather vest. When he used the whip, his muscles bulged. Rich stopped dead and growled when he saw who had come in.

"What the fuck are you doin' here?" Rich demanded.

"I could ask you the same thing," Dmitri said blandly, hearing the door close behind him while he examined every detail around them, looking for threats and weapons.

"*I'm* here with Alex," Rich growled. "I rode up with her, so I'm invited. You're not. In fact you gotta lotta balls to be up here, considering you're on the run from the cops."

"What makes you think I'm on the run?"

Dmitri moved over to lean against a bale of hay, appearing to be totally relaxed and at ease, while staying alert to any movement the other man might make.

"You ran outta Tom's wake like your ass was on fire when the detective showed up. Oh, that's right. You're illegal, aren't you? But that's not the only reason you ran, I'll bet."

"Oh? Why else do you think I'd be avoiding the authorities?"

"Cause you're ex-KGB, right? Probably got cops all over the world looking for you. Only this time you're going down."

"For something I didn't do? You're a lot dumber than I thought if you think I'm afraid of some two-bit hustler who thinks he's hot-shit because he enjoys violence."

Rich growled and advanced, still holding the whip.

"What're you going to do with that whip, dude? Going to draw blood on a man? I thought you were more into hurting women before you fuck them. Kind of softens them up. They're so grateful you stopped hitting them, they act like they're enjoying you."

"What the fuck are you talking about? Who told you that?"

Dmitri smirked. "Who do you think? Alexandra told me a lot about all of her guys. That's why when the murders started,

I knew it had to be you doing it. You're the one who likes violence so much the rest of the gang's been wanting to throw you out for a while. Too bad they didn't, 'cause then Tom and Jim would still be alive."

"You'd know about that, asshole. Since you're the one who killed them."

Dmitri shook his head. "Nah. You did. And you wanna know how I knew it was you?"

Rich stood still but everything about his stance suggested he was coiling himself like a spring, getting ready to attack. Dmitri braced himself while continuing to give the appearance of being relaxed.

"Everyone in the bar knew Tom always ran outta cigarettes sometime during long Friday night parties. He'd always run across the street to the gas station. It wouldn't have been hard for you to hide the rental car somewhere nearby, then go to the can right after he headed out. You snuck out the back door, got into the car and ran him down. You hid the car then went back in through the back door while everyone was out front, and when you appeared you could say you were in the can so you missed all of the action." Dmitri stopped talking and smiled at Rich. "Am I right so far?"

"Like you said, everyone knew that. So you could have just pretended to be out of town and done that. It's your word against mine and I'm a citizen...you're not."

Dmitri nodded. "Ah, but you're forgetting I have no idea where Jim worked. So I'd have no way of knowing where his territory was, or where he always made deliveries on Saturday afternoons. That was only known to the long-time members... like you."

Rich grunted. "But the cops talked to the rental place guy. That's how they figured out it was you."

"And how would he point them to me?"

"The accent. The guy who rented the car had your accent."

Dmitri stared at Rich who looked triumphant, like he'd won the argument.

"Dew yew mean y'all cain't thank of me doin' eny other kand of accaint? Sure'n Alex me luv kin tell ye aboot the miny accents and brogues ah kin do. In fact, you stupid asshole, I can do lots of accents in at least five different languages. Why the fuck would I use my own accent, to point the finger right back at me?" Dmitri smiled at the surprised look on Rich's face. "And besides, how did you know about any accent used by the guy who rented the car? The owner only told that to the police. And they only shared that with Alex, and I know she didn't share that with you."

With a roar, Rich hurled himself across the space between them and tried to wrestle Dmitri to the ground. Dmitri had seen the tensing of his legs and was expecting the advance. They were evenly-matched in height and strength, with Rich's street-fighting skills a match for Dmitri's years of training.

Both got in some hits, both did some blocking. Rich fought in a blind rage, while Dmitri held back so he didn't kill his opponent.

I want him arrested, not dead. Where the hell are the cops who were supposed to be hiding in here? They must have heard him confess...

Suddenly Alexandra threw open the barn door and screamed, "He's got a knife, Dmitri!"

For an instant Dmitri lost his concentration as he yelled at her, "Get out of here!"

He felt the knife slice into his abdomen and Rich tried to jerk it upwards through his ribs to his heart. Dmitri placed a hand on the wound to try and stop the bleeding. As he tried to dislodge the knife, Rich slashed at his hand. Dmitri lashed out, disabling his attacker with the same punch to the diaphragm he'd used on Jim in the bar on his first visit there.

Rich staggered backwards and passed out in a pile of hay. Dmitri fell to his knees, blood streaming from his wound, as he tried to hold back the bleeding with his shirt.

Alexandra rushed over to fall to her knees in front of him.

"Oh God, Dmitri! Let me help you..."

That was the moment the police chose to make their presence known.

Detective Jones strode over to where Alexandra tried to stanch the blood streaming from Dmitri's wound.

"We got their words on tape. We've already called for an ambulance. Since there's no hospital close enough, they're sending out a helicopter. But for now please move out of the way. Officer Strung is a trained EMT."

Alexandra looked up at the officer who already had gloves on and was setting a med-kit down next to Dmitri who was now sitting, having fallen back from his knees. He swayed slightly as his hand was pulled away from the wound. The sheer amount of blood-loss made him dizzy. Immediately the officer applied clean cloths to the wound, pressing down while she directed another officer to cut tape strips to hold the cloths in place.

"I don't want to leave him," Alexandra said in a strained voice as Detective Jones pulled her up to stand on her feet.

"You can't help him anymore right now," he said evenly.

"Dmitri, I won't leave you. I'll be by your side," she said hoping for a response.

Dmitri nodded his head weakly, "I know…"

His eyes rolled back in his head and he fell backwards as he passed out. The EMT efficiently continued to tend to the wound.

"Detective Jones? He's waking up," an officer said from behind them.

Both the detective and Alexandra turned around to see that Rich had been pulled to his feet and was being cuffed by one officer.

Detective Jones walked over to say, "Rich Montreau, I'm putting you under arrest for the murders of Tom Taylor and Jim Richmond. Officer, read him his rights." He turned back to where he expected Alexandra to be standing.

Alexandra walked up close to where Rich stood. He stared around groggily as he recovered from the loss of oxygen that had made him pass out.

Suddenly her right fist shot out and she punched him in the groin. He yelped as she crushed his genitals, then her other fist shot up and punched his windpipe.

She snarled at him, "That first one is from Jim. He taught me how to do that sucker-punch, you shit-head. The second one is from Tom, who taught me how to do that one. You are a twisted fuck and I should have thrown you out with the garbage years ago. I'll feel guilty forever that they paid the price of my stupidity."

"I…did…it…for…you…" He had to struggle against the pain to make his words barely audible. "You an' me…"

"There *never* was any *you and me*. I don't ever want to see you again. You're a waste of skin."

Detective Jones pulled her back, holding both of her arms in a lock behind her.

"Miss Blackstone, you can't abuse him. He's under arrest. We can't risk the case being thrown out due to claims of police violence."

"You're not being violent," she snapped, "I am."

The sounds of a helicopter drowned out the detective's response as it landed in the yard. Two more EMTs entered the barn with a stretcher and moved Dmitri onto it for transport.

Alexandra turned back to the still-moaning Rich who had fallen to his knees but been pulled back up by two officers. She tried to shrug off the hold the detective had on her, but he was determined to keep her still.

"You'd better hope he doesn't die, you piece of shit. Because if he does, I don't care what kind of deep, dark hole they throw your worthless ass into. I'll find you and kill you myself."

As Dmitri was carried out of the barn, Alexandra struggled to move again.

"Can't I go with him?" She asked the detective who held her immobile.

"You promise not to hit anyone again?"

She nodded. "Yes."

He called to the EMTs, "Is there room in the helicopter for a passenger?"

"Probably," one called out as they moved through the door.

"Go," Detective Jones said as he released her arms. "We'll bring your things to you at the hospital after we get him out of here."

Alexandra took off at a sprint after Dmitri and ran to the helicopter. An officer helped her to climb up into it and once she sat by Dmitri's head, out of the way of the busy med-techs, the pilot took them up into the air.

Alexandra smoothed back a lock of Dmitri's black hair that had fallen on his forehead.

"Please, please, please, God," she whispered, "Don't take him away from me. I can be a better woman with him in my life. Please give me that chance..."

Chapter Sixteen

The next day in late afternoon, Emma knocked quietly on the hospital room door and when there was no answer, she pushed it open. The first thing she saw was Dmitri in the bed hooked up to various medical devices. She looked around further and saw Alexandra snoring softly on the chair next to the bed, still in the blood-covered clothes she'd worn in the barn, her head dropped down on her chest. She walked over to the chair, dropped a backpack on the floor and reached over to pat her friend on the side of the face.

"Alex?" she asked quietly. "Alex, honey, I brought you the stuff you asked for."

Alexandra sighed as she opened her eyes and looked towards Dmitri, who still hadn't moved.

"He's not awake yet, is he?" Emma said with sympathy.

Alexandra shook her head, her eyes suddenly filled with the tears so uncommon to her.

"He'll be fine. The nurse told me he's pulling through okay. He's just resting now. I'm more worried about you."

"Why?" She had to cough to clear her throat, her voice harsh from the ordeal she'd been through, as well as sleeping in the dry environment of a hospital.

"You haven't been eating or sleeping. You haven't left his side for twenty-four hours. If you're not going to work tomorrow, you need to call your office and let them know you won't be in. I called your Dad like you asked me to and he's coming here later tonight after he's done golfing, according to your stepmother. At least take a shower and change into something that won't fry your dad's brain when he walks into the room."

Alexandra turned to look at her friend and Emma was struck by how haunted and sad her friend's eyes looked. The confidence and swagger that normally emanated from such a strong woman was replaced with worry and anxiety.

"I don't care. I'm not leaving Dmitri until he wakes up and I know he's okay."

"I can sit here with him and wait while you shower and change," Emma suggested.

"No!"

Emma shrugged. "Okay. I'm going downstairs to get you some coffee and something to eat. I'll be back soon."

She leaned over to give her friend a brief kiss on the cheek, then turned and left them alone again.

Alexandra moved her chair closer to the bed and patted Dmitri's hand that was closest to her and didn't have IV tubes attached to it.

She stared at his face, looking for any signs of returning consciousness.

Please, please, please come back to me! Give me the chance to tell you what I've never told any man!

She leaned her head over and rested her cheek against the back of his hand. Tears streamed silently out of her eyes as she tried to remember how to pray.

She thought she imagined the touch of an angel as a hand rested on her head, then gently stroked her hair, until she realized whose hand it was and lifted her head to look into his eyes.

"Dmitri! You're awake!"

He nodded. "Yuh." then coughed and lifted an eyebrow. "Water?"

She stood and picked up the paper cup with a straw in it from off the bedside table, and held the straw to his lips. He took a few sips, swallowed, then his eyes closed again. She studied his face until his eyes opened to look into hers.

"How long?"

"Twenty-four hours, give or take."

"Rich?"

"In jail, accused of two murders."

He nodded his head slightly. "Good."

"Detective Jones said he wants to talk to you when you wake up, but that might not be until tomorrow. But my dad will be coming over later tonight."

A flash of anxiety flitted across his face as he asked, "Are there guards outside the door?"

Alexandra blinked in surprise. "Uh, no. Should there be?"

"If my ID wasn't good, there would be." He smiled, closed his eyes again and sighed with satisfaction. "Good."

She watched as a grimace of pain replaced the smile.

"Should I call for a nurse? You look like you're in pain..."

"I am. But not just yet. Now I'm here legally, I want to ask you something."

"You do?"

He nodded. "Can I have more water?"

She held the straw to his lips again and he swallowed a few more times.

He took a deep breath. "Alexandra Blackstone, will you do me the honor of becoming my wife?"

Alexandra coughed in surprise. "*What*? You almost died and that's the first thing you want to ask me?"

His lips curved upwards. "Of course! Near-death experiences always make it clear what really matters. If you will be my wife, I'll have everything I want to be a happy man. So, yes or no?"

"You ask me that *now*? While I look like hell? With my eyes all puffy from crying over you...and I smell bad from wearing these blood-covered clothes for too long?"

"My blood...from when you tried to save me," he observed. "That makes it a badge of honor from one warrior to another."

"I punched him after you passed out. The detective had to pull me off him. I punched him in the groin for Jim and in the throat for Tom."

"Good. I'd expect nothing less from my fiery biker queen."

"I told him if you died, I'd hunt him down and kill him myself."

"I hope the police weren't taping that part..." he said dryly.

"I didn't care. All I could think of was how I would feel if I lost you. Tom and Jim died because I didn't throw that piece of shit out of the gang when we all knew how violent he was. I actually thought about it a few times, but I figured that since his violence was really helpful when we got into it with other gangs, that it was okay to let him stay. And some of the gals kind of like some brutality with their sex, though that's never been my thing."

"Lots of guys are violent, given the opportunity. You couldn't have known how much he was obsessing over you. He saw a chance to get you for himself by making me take the blame."

"But it's my fault they're dead! I thought I was bad-ass enough to keep all of the guys in line. The truth is, I don't feel very bad-ass anymore. All I've been doing is crying for the past twenty-four hours...and begging God to let you live."

Her words ended on a sob. She took several deep breaths trying to calm down.

Dmitri patted the hand that rested on his bed, while she wiped her eyes with the other one.

"This isn't my first brush with death, *Sashka*," he said gently. "God and I are on pretty good terms."

"You got distracted when I went into the barn...so it's my fault you got stabbed..." Her words ended on another sob, as if she was being crushed under the guilt.

"No, *Sashka*," he corrected her, "I knew he had the knife. I was waiting for him to pull it and trying not to kill him because the cops were watching. But when I saw you walk in, all I thought of was getting you safely out of there. It's my own fault for being so careless. Don't blame yourself...I don't."

He watched her shudder as she tried to stop sobbing. He shook his head gently. "Don't, *Sashka*. Don't blame yourself for any of this. Or if you have to, let me absolve you of the guilt. Or go to confession...do anything you have to do to let yourself feel better."

She looked up and tried to smile, "I'm not Catholic. We don't do confession."

"Then what are you?"

"Duh! I'm born and raised in Minnesota, so I'm a Lutheran, of course. Lapsed, but that's what I was raised."

Dmitri tried to shrug. "I guess I can convert...or you can. But honey, no one could have known he was going to act out his worst impulses. Most guys, even those with major power and violence issues, never take the final step to murder. I probably should have been more on my guard around all of your men, but my head wasn't in the game the way it should be. I was too busy falling in love with their queen."

She stopped crying and studied his face intently.

"Which reminds me, you haven't answered my question yet. I'm not going to let you call for a nurse yet, even though I could really use the pain relief, until you do. So this literally is hurting me more than it's hurting you, but I have to know."

She opened her mouth but nothing came out.

"Sashka," he began, "I'm a long way from where I was born. I've lived on almost all of the continents and done things even I don't want to remember. I've been on the move for many, many years...and for most of them I've been happy to be that way. But now I've found a reason to want to stay in one place. That reason is you. I need to know if you feel the same about me. Or should I keep on moving?"

She swallowed hard, tears welling up in her eyes again.

"Look at me! I'm like a love-struck teenager who can't stop crying. Dmitri, I don't care about anything else. I want to have you with me, always. I guess I'll have to give up having other men, since that's a part of the whole marriage bargain thing, right?"

His lips curled upwards. "Um...yeah, that's actually the most important part...to me, anyway."

"Yes, I'll marry you. I don't care when or where. But I will because I...because..." She looked embarrassed, glancing around the room while he waited silently and patiently.

"Because I...I love you, Dmitri. I've never told any man that, ever. I've always been afraid of how much power that gives you over me. But I don't care. I give you that power. I love you."

He held out his free arm and she moved forward to put her arms around his shoulders and they held each other for a long moment made awkward by the hospital bed sides and the IV tubes inhibiting his movement. His free hand moved up and into her hair and he inhaled deeply, then exhaled on a long sigh. "Okay, *now*, Sashka? Could you please call for the nurse to bring me some pain meds now?"

She backed up to give him a lop-sided grin, "You mean my love isn't all you need?"

He grimaced back at her. "It will be once my wound heals. But for now, it burns like a bitch and I'd really like some drugs."

"Aren't you supposed to kiss me now I've said yes? To seal the bargain and all?"

"Bring your lips back down here."

She leaned over and their lips met, a gentle brush against each other. Then she stood up and pressed the button to call the nurse.

When the nurse walked in, she bustled around angrily, upset she hadn't been summoned the instant he was awake and irritated that Alexandra still hadn't changed out of the unsanitary blood-soaked clothing she'd been wearing for far too long.

While Dmitri's vitals were checked, Emma came back into

the room with the coffee and a bagel. The nurse shooed them both out of the room.

"Go on, get out of here, both of you! I need to change the dressing on his wound so you need to leave. And before you come back in here, young lady," she said pointedly to Alexandra, "You need to get out of those filthy clothes."

Meekly Alexandra nodded and picked up the backpack Emma had dropped on the floor. They went down the hall to find the shower room.

* * * *

The word *gang* was never used when they told Thomas Blackstone about his daughter's friends being hunted by a man who committed murder, implicating Dmitri because he was jealous and wanted her to himself. He seemed dazed at the idea that his daughter, in whom he had invested so much time and energy to teach her how to run his business, had been in danger. When she made it clear Dmitri was willing to risk his life to bring the murderer to justice, Alexandra watched as her father beamed at the injured man.

Dmitri had eaten some bland food and had a cup of coffee, so he looked to be on his way to a full recovery. His voice sounded stronger, partly due to the drugs he had talked the nurse into adding to his IV. When there was a lull in the conversation, Dmitri cleared his throat.

"There's a couple of things we need to tell you about, sir," he addressed her father formally which made the man's eyebrows raise in surprise.

"Please, Dmitri, there's no need for such formality. You kept my daughter safe. There's nothing you could ask that I would deny."

"That's actually a very good thing, since I've asked her to marry me. I don't know if you want me to formally ask you for her hand, but if you do, I'm doing it now."

Thomas turned to stare intently at his daughter, who was busy squirming in her seat over his scrutiny as she always had done since she was a child.

"Oh? And what did you answer him, Alex?"

"I said yes, Dad."

He smiled broadly. "You did? Excellent! Then I can rest easy knowing there's a man taking care of you."

Alexandra bristled. "Now Dad, it's the twenty-first century, you know. I can take care of myself."

"Yes, I know you can. But still, it's nice to know you've got such a big, strong man to guard your back."

She stuck out her tongue at her father and he grinned back at her.

Dmitri cleared his throat again. "And that's not all. I bring a wedding gift of business to the company. The conglomerate of Russian manufacturers I told you about has asked me to represent their interests introducing their products to this market, and I can't think of a better firm to represent them than yours."

"When you get out of the hospital, Dmitri, I insist on you two being my guests at a party I'll throw for you at the club. I want to introduce you to all of my business contacts, to let them know the good news."

"Aren't you upset I'm going to be getting married, like any other woman?" Alexandra persisted. "You never treated me like I was a woman before."

Her father stared at her. "How did I treat you?"

"Like some kind of neuter. Not quite a man, but not a woman, because you've never had much respect for them."

He continued to look into her eyes for a long time before he sighed heavily.

"I know you were disappointed in me when I divorced your mother to marry Abby. I didn't realize how much it affected you until years later. And then it was too late to even bring it up with you. Yes, I treated you like the son I never had, because I wanted to leave my business to someone in the family. You took to marketing and sales like you had been born to do it. You also have a ruthless streak that makes you the best possible choice for leading my firm. But I never wanted that to stop you from having a life of your own. That's why I never asked about your Harley hobby. I bought you your first one, if you remember."

She nodded. "Yes, you did."

"So, let me be happy for you. You've found yourself a good man who will take care of you when you need it." He noticed her beginning to bristle again and quickly added, "And you'll take care of him when he needs it, like you're doing now. It's a two-way street, Alex. I've learned there are times when a man needs to lean on someone too. It's been a hard lesson for a stubborn old coot like me, but I'm trying to keep an open mind."

"An open mind, huh?" Alexandra asked. "Then will you invite Mom to the engagement celebration party at the club?"

He looked into her eyes. "Will that make you happy?"

She nodded.

"Then yes. I'll invite your sister and her brood as well. Hopefully she'll be smart enough to hire a baby-sitter for the kids, but with her...who knows?"

They chatted comfortably for a while after that. When the nurse came in to announce that visiting hours were ending, Thomas Blackstone rose to leave.

"I'll drop by your office tomorrow morning and let them know you're not going to be in. You can decide when you want to return. Take your time. After all, other than a day or two to extend weekends here and there, you haven't really taken any vacation time for years. And don't argue with me. I have my sources. I still keep tabs on what's going on. It's just I haven't had any complaints, so I never needed to let you know that. But the company won't fail if you take a few days off to be with your man. You've hired good people to help you run it. Let them take over until you feel up to going back."

"Thanks, Dad. I'm sure I'll be back soon."

Thomas Blackstone turned at the door to smile at them both, "And Dmitri? Welcome to the family...son."

Once the door closed, Alexandra scooted her chair over to be closer to Dmitri.

"That went well," Dmitri remarked.

"Yeah, much better than I expected. He didn't ask many questions about what went on, though."

Dmitri grinned. "I'll bet he decided a long time ago he didn't want to know the answers to any questions about your personal life. So he just didn't ask. He did appear pleased that you and I are going to be married."

"Yeah, but he expects that things will go on as usual, and I'll keep running the company."

"You will. There's no reason for you not to."

"Are you going to move into my condo with me?"

"I suppose I will. I *do* like the amenities." He waited a heartbeat before continuing with his teasing, "And the Jacuzzi and workout room are great too."

"Oh? So now my pussy is part of the *amenities*? I should make you eat those words."

"I'd rather eat your pussy."

She raised both eyebrows. "You're not feeling *that* much better yet, are you? Because as soon as you are, you just let me know, big guy."

"Not yet, sweetheart. But as soon as I am, I'll show you. But there was something else I've been thinking about..."

She leaned closer to stare into his eyes. "What?"

"Remember I told you I grew up on a farm?"

"Yes."

"Your grandparents used to farm the land around your place, didn't they?"

"Yes. I remember eating fresh corn that I helped pick, and eating jams and pies made from the fruit from their orchard, when I was a kid."

"Well I was thinking that if I moved out there and lived there during the growing season, you could come out on weekends to be with me. Or I could drive in to be with you in your condo. But I'd like a chance to do some farming myself. And the growing season isn't that long this far north, so most of the year I'd be in the condo with you."

She stared into his face. "You really have thought about this, haven't you?"

"Yes. For a while we'll keep it really small...maybe just a garden at first. But eventually I'd like to try some real farming. I used to be really good at it, from what my Dad used to tell me."

He smiled at the look on her face. He reached up with the arm not attached to hospital equipment and pulled her down for a long, sensual kiss.

"And when we're ready for a child, if I'm farming the land, I could be a stay-at-home father. You could work at home a few days a week, once we get internet access out on the farm, then drive in to stay at your condo a few days. Then come back to home-cooked meals and a real family-life on your farm. What do you think of that idea, *Sashka*?"

She backed up to stare at him intently.

"You mean to say you want to marry me, but I can keep on working? And if I get pregnant..."

"*When* you get pregnant," he corrected gently.

"You'll be the one to stay at home and I can keep on running my company?"

He nodded. "Yes. Does that sound alright to you?"

There were tears in her eyes as she nodded.

"Oh, my God, Dmitri! All of this time I thought I would never get married because no man could satisfy all of my demands. Then you came along and proved that you were man enough for me. I was so afraid that no man would allow me to keep working, that if the guy was alpha enough to go toe-to-toe with me and hold his own, that he'd insist I stay at home with the baby. But that's not what you're saying, is it? And somehow, thinking of you holding a baby is making me hotter than anything else I've ever imagined!"

He smiled as he stroked the back of her hand. "That's just because it's been a few days and we're both really horny."

He almost laughed at the hopeful look that appeared on her face.

"No, I told you, I'm not ready yet. But soon, *Sashka*...soon. And when I plunge myself into you again, it will be the first time as your only man. I intend to savor that moment. Because you are mine, Alexandra Blackstone. From now on, only one man has access to your body."

She smiled as she nodded. "That's right, Dmitri. From now on, only one man will do for me. Because you're the only man I could ever have said yes to. You're not trying to change me. You're not trying to make me into something I'm not."

"No. I want you to continue being the fiery, independent, stubborn wildcat I came here to tame. You're not ever going to heel for me, and that's okay. The challenge of mating with you is part of the attraction. As long as we both understand that you belong to me, and I belong to you, then I'm happy."

Alexandra leaned over for a very long, almost full body snuggle with Dmitri, during which he fondled her ass with his one good hand and managed to get a squeeze in on both of her breasts. She moved her hand down to hold his semi-turgid cock, stroking it until it threatened to get serious. He used the hand with the IV attached to hit her hand away.

"Mercy, woman! Let me heal. We have the rest of our lives for enjoying each other. And besides, you don't want to have the hospital reporting they had to throw you out for molesting a convalescing patient, do you?"

She shook her head. "No."

"Then go home and get some rest. If I can, I'll badger them into letting me go home with you tomorrow night. You may need to consider taking the next day off of work as well. So we can have some time to...ahem...get reacquainted."

Alexandra smiled as she straightened up and stuffed her breasts back into position in her bra. She turned to pick up her backpack and headed out the door.

"Dream of me?" she asked as she turned the handle to go out.

"Of course. Think of me when you're *doing yourself* with that huge dildo of yours?"

She turned and gaped at him, and he grinned.

"I'm a trained agent. I always check out any place I'm spending time in. And I might add, it's *almost* as big as I am. So go have your fun. Keep it hot and juicy for me."

Alexandra stuck her tongue out at him, then curled it back repeatedly like she was licking him, until he moaned.

"Have mercy!"

"Never!" Her laughter could be heard from down the hall as she swung her hips and headed out.

Epilogue

Raul Roderick, the most famous resident of Grand Marais, Minnesota pushed open the door to call into the resort, "Ivan? It's me, Raul."

Looking into the small liquor store on the one side, he saw no one there and the door locked, so he headed up the stairs. He was almost knocked over by two excitable dogs that galloped around the corners at the top of the stairs and tried to attack him with joy at his arrival while he was still walking up.

"Down, boys! Yes, I'm happy to see you too! Both of you! Now if I pet you both on the head and scratch behind your ears, will you let Ivan know I'm here?"

He stooped down once he was on the second floor and made sure to give equal pets to both of Ivan's spoiled babies. When he thought he had given them sufficient attention, he straightened and looked around while clapping his hands together to dislodge the hair the dogs had gifted him with.

The dining room was empty, but then since it was midafternoon, he'd been expecting that. The lunch crowd was long gone and most were out fishing, hiking, swimming, or enjoying any of the other outdoor amenities to be had up in the gorgeous natural splendor of the Boundary Waters Canoe Area of northern Minnesota. He took a moment to admire the view from the dining room of the lake behind the resort.

Hearing the crack of pool balls from a table in the bar off to the side of the dining room, he headed through the doorway to see who was there. When he saw the red hair he stopped as if he'd been struck by lightning. His pulse and breathing sped up, and suddenly he felt like he was in a nightmare where he was terrified, but unable to move.

The woman looked up from lining up a shot and smirked.

"Jesus, they let anyone in around here, don't they? Will you look what the cat dragged in? If it isn't Raul Roderick, the rich and famous, incredibly hot, Oscar-winning, action-movie star."

Raul felt rooted to the spot though his heart was racing and his brain was trying to tell his feet to run away quickly. They ignored the order. His mouth gaped open and it didn't respond to his orders for it to close, let alone make words come out.

The woman finished lining up another shot and sunk the ball using two banks, before she looked up.

"Nice to meet you again. You're much better looking when you're not totally wasted. Long time no see, huh? How the hell are you?"

"Uh...fine. Um...what're you doing here?"

She aimed and shot another perfect bank shot, then stopped to chalk her cue while she grinned.

"I'm *not* here looking for you, so you can stop hyper-ventilating. Maybe you should sit down with your head between your legs? You look like you're gonna pass out, big guy. You want a paper bag to breathe into?"

"You're not?"

"No. You had Ivan send his cousin to be sure I wouldn't come looking for you, remember? I mean it *was* a while ago, but now you've cleaned up your act, I'd think you'd remember that night we met."

She laughed, a low, throaty chuckle that made his hair stand on end.

"Then, why're you here?"

She took another shot that sunk two balls in order, then looked up at him.

"When you had Ivan send his cousin after me, you actually did me a favor. If there's ever anything I can do to repay that, you just let me know."

She winked and Raul was horrified to feel a blush burning his face.

"He found you?"

She nodded and sunk the last ball on a three-bank shot.

"Yeah, he found me alright."

She straightened up and rubbed her belly to draw his attention away from her massive cleavage to the swelling under her loosely-draped shirt. He gaped.

"The proof is in the Russian *kolatchy* in my oven. And this," she waved her left hand to show him the wedding ring.

"*Kolatchy* is a *Polish* cookie, Alexandra."

Raul jumped as a man's voice came from behind him. The

man in question walked over to pick up his glass from the bar and take a long drink of water.

"So, what *would* you call this?" she demanded.

The man shrugged casually. "A *babka*?"

"Fine. Whatever you call it, it's getting huge and pushy in there," she said testily. "Good thing you're back. I was just gonna call you anyway."

The man's lips curved upwards. "Why? Did you finally miss a shot so I can have a turn?"

She shook her head. "No. I cleaned up the table again. But I'm gonna rack 'em up and let you have the first shot again."

She proceeded to do just that, moving all around the table to roll the balls to the one end.

"If she didn't let me have the first shot, I'd never get to play at all," the man said conversationally to Raul before he stuck out his hand for a shake. "I'm Dmitri Illyanovich. One of Ivan's cousins."

Raul was finally able to move so he shook the man's hand.

"Raul Roderick," he said, glad his body was responding to commands again.

"He knows who you are, you idiot," the redhead remarked with snark. "After all, you're the reason he came looking for me."

"No, my love. It was fate that drew me to your location, so I could orbit your magnificence like a hopeless planet caught by the gravity of a super-nova."

She snorted rudely. "What horseshit!" She finished racking up the balls and looked expectantly over at Dmitri.

"You never did learn her name, did you?" he asked Raul as she watched them.

"Come over here and rest for a minute, *Sashka*. You need to stay hydrated since it's so damned hot today. Honestly, the real reason Ivan moved up here, besides the remoteness, is that the climate is usually more like Mother Russia: cold, snowy, icy winds. The best of everything. But the summers can be unbearable."

The redhead walked over to sit on the bar stool next to him and as she got closer, Raul saw just how very pregnant she looked.

"Raul, this is my wife, the former Alexandra Blackstone. Now Alexandra Illyanovich. Make nice with the actor, honey. He's still afraid of you. Show him you're not dangerous anymore."

She turned to Raul and bared her teeth to growl. Raul grinned, still not totally at ease yet.

"Honestly? Since I can't drink alcohol to kill my pain, I'm really suffering! This baby-making thing sounds like a good idea until you're actually doing it. The early part wasn't so bad, but this is getting more uncomfortable by the day."

She punched Dmitri's upper arm.

"How about *you* have the next one...deal?"

Raul smiled. "My wife says if everyone was as uncomfortable during the whole time as they are during the last month or so, we'd all be only children. Speaking as an only child, I'm really grateful that nature gives you amnesia about the end once you hold the baby for the first time."

Alexandra studied his face as he was talking.

"Is that the same woman you blew me off for?" She rolled her eyes. "Lucky gal. So how many rug rats has she popped out for you?"

"We have twin sons and she's pregnant for the second time."

"Congratulations." Dmitri clapped him on the shoulder in the kind of gesture he'd grown to expect from Ivan. "Sons to carry on the name!"

"Ahem. Not to interrupt the testosterone-fest or anything, but daughters can do that too. And run your company when you retire."

"Of course they can," Dmitri said in a conciliatory tone. "Would you like more iced water?"

"No, what I'd really like is a beer. But yeah, pour me another glass. I've gotta go pee. I'll be right back."

They watched her leave, then Dmitri turned to Raul with a grin.

"She's not always this bad-tempered. Not being able to drink has lost its novelty appeal to her and she's getting very uncomfortable...especially with the heat and humidity these days. That's why I asked Ivan if we could come up here to relax for a few days. She runs her father's marketing company and doesn't plan on stopping until she delivers. I keep telling her she's pushing herself too hard, but she's a very stubborn woman."

Raul nodded. "I can still see signs she's the biker queen of my nightmares. But she does seem to have mellowed a little bit."

"I don't want her to change too much. I love her the way she is. She's tough as nails with an independent streak a mile wide. But no matter how many scars I have from tangling with her, I'm happy she's *my* wildcat."

"Even if she always beats you at pool?"

Dmitri shrugged. "You should have seen how bad I was when I first met her. I'm learning more each time I play with her. One of these days I'm gonna win a game. The celebrating will be legendary."

Raul grinned at the look of anticipation on Dmitri's face.

"Ah, there you are, Raul! I have been looking for you! Muddy and Buddy came bounding over to let me know you had arrived."

Ivan pulled Raul off the bar stool for a huge bear hug. The actor had obviously become accustomed to this greeting, because he braced himself so he never lost his balance despite Ivan's effusive enthusiasm.

"I see you two have met? Good...good." He turned to Dmitri. "And where is that firecracker of a wife of yours?"

"Right here. I'm so fucking hot and uncomfortable I think I *will* take you up on the offer to go swimming, Dmitri. Maybe if I can cool off a little bit, I'll be able to stand waiting until dinner for my one beer of the day."

The other two men watched Dmitri as he stood up.

"Gentlemen? You'll have to pardon me while I go admire my wife's ass in a bathing suit."

"Admire? I look like a whale!"

"Ah, but remember how you got to look like that, my love?"

Suddenly her face changed to a mixture of love and lust. Even Raul had to admit that when not snarling or angry, she was a beautiful woman.

"Yeah," she said. "Dmitri, I think I'll need your help getting into my maternity suit." She winked broadly at him.

He strode over to give her a quick kiss. "Your wish is my command."

As they walked out holding hands, Ivan moved behind the bar to pour two drafts. He slid them both onto the bar and walked back to sit next to Raul. They clinked their glasses together before both took a long drink of the cold lagers.

"You see, my friend," Ivan said as he nodded in the direction of the exit. "I told you everything would work out for you."

Raul smiled. "That was the best wedding present you could have given me, Ivan."

They clinked their glasses together again.

"It seems to have worked out well for them also," Raul observed. "Now we have to find a woman for you."

Ivan's laughter was loud and infectious.

"I'm in no hurry, my friend. This country has given me so much already. I can wait."

"You think she's just going to walk in through your door someday?"

Ivan smiled. "Da. Someday she will. And I'll be here waiting for her."

With that issue settled, they resumed discussing the publicity Raul was going to do for Ivan's resort, and the work that two of Ivan's other cousins were doing on Raul's mansion on the hill.

About the Author:

Fiona has always had stories in her head. Characters intrude into her thoughts and insist on showing her scenes from their lives. She discovered that when she ignores them, they start to yell louder; if she writes their stories and they can live in readers' heads as well, they usually leave her alone...only to be replaced by a new group of story-tellers. Her head is usually a very crowded place, but she likes it that way.

If you want to read more, she has a series of six contemporary romance books about the members of a large Hispanic family. She wrote two books about female spies who work for a top-secret international agency, as well as two stand-alone contemporary romances. She has also written two paranormal erotic romance books about Mayan vampires.

Visit her at: http://www.fionamcgier.com, where the first page is her blog.

She also blogs at:
http://www.sweetnsexydivas.blogspot.com

Other Titles by Fiona McGier:
Prophecy of the Undead
Mayan Prophecy Fulfilled
For the Love of His Life

Also from Eternal Press:

For the Love of His Life
by Fiona McGier

eBook ISBN: 9781615729210
Print ISBN: 9781615729227

Contemporary Romance
Novel of 81,229 words

Can a sexy Hispanic action movie star find himself in the BWCA of upper Minnesota? Will the local woman he grows to love believe someone who "lies for a living"?

When a famous action star needs to clean-up for a major role that even he doubts he can deliver, the director sends him up to a resort owned by his grandmother in the Boundary Waters Canoe Area of upper Minnesota, to learn to commune with nature. His guide is Veronica, the director's cousin, a tall, athletic woman who has the relaxed, sensible nature of someone who knows herself well. Raul's initial clumsy attempt to seduce her makes her laugh...so he calls her fat. There may be hope that their relationship will progress beyond its rocky start. Raul must overcome his partying nature to discover what is really important in life.

Also from Eternal Press:

Mommy Blogger
by Carla Caruso

eBook ISBN: 9781615727223
Print ISBN: 9781615727230

Contemporary Romance, Humor
Novel of 68,698 words

One baby, one lie—and a whole new career. Stella lands a great job as a mommy blogger. The catch is she's never had children. Plunged into a world of insanity every mother faces, she must learn to cope as her lies build upon one another. A sexy ex comes into the picture, forcing her to choose between him or the job and a handsome 'keeper' of a coworker. It can't last forever.

Eternal Press

Official Website:
http://www.eternalpress.biz

Blog:
http://www.eternalpress.biz/blog/

Reader Chat Group:
http://groups.yahoo.com/group/EternalPressReaders

Twitter:
http://twitter.com/EternalPress

Facebook:
http://www.facebook.com/profile.php?id=1364272754

Google +:
https://plus.google.com/u/0/115524941844122973800

Good Reads:
http://www.goodreads.com/profile/EternalPress

Shelfari:
http://www.shelfari.com/eternalpress

Library Thing:
http://www.librarything.com/catalog/EternalPress

We invite you to drop in, visit with our authors, and stay in touch for the latest news, releases, and more!

CPSIA information can be obtained at www.ICGtesting.com
Printed in the USA
LVOW11s2024071213

364321LV00001B/1/P